My Big Gay
Family Christmas
Wedding Disaster

ALEX LESLIE

Published by Alex Leslie, 2024

MY BIG GAY FAMILY CHRISTMAS WEDDING DISASTER
First Edition: November 30, 2024
Copyright © 2024 Alex Leslie

This is a work of fiction. Names, characters, places, and incidents either are products of the author's imagination or used fictitiously. Any resemblance to actual persons, living or dead, business establishments, events or locales is entirely coincidental.

Cover Art Design by https://selfpubbookcovers.com/PremiumRomance

Cover content is for illustrative purposes only. Any person depicted on the cover is a model.

This work is written by an Australian author in Australian English. It features several examples of commonplace Australian terms, references, colloquialisms and spelling.

If you enjoy this book, please consider rating it and writing a review. Reviews help readers discover new books and help keep artists motivated to produce new work.

Any unauthorised reproduction or distribution of this work is a violation of applicable copyright laws. Also, I will place a curse on any possessors of pirated material. Okay, I won't put a curse on you. I'm not that powerful. But I'll think about cursing you *really* hard and hope that such action will somehow allow me to manifest the ability to curse people. If it works, you're in for a whole world of trouble, buddy

Seriously, though. Don't steal books. It's bad. Plus it makes authors give up on writing. Then you'll run out of books to steal.

Prologue – Shifty Mother Is Shifty

SHE'S GONE INSANE.

That was the only possible explanation I could come up with for my mother's recent peculiar behaviour. For the last couple of days, my Mum had been calling and texting me multiple times a day and at all hours of the day and night. She has been asking me a series of seemingly random and increasingly strange questions. She would use text to ask anything that only required a quick, one-word answer, such as asking me what my favourite colour was. For anything requiring a more in-depth answer, Kathleen Nolan would contact me directly on the phone and refuse to hang up until I answered her questions to her satisfaction. Some curious highlights of my mother's mysterious one-woman inquisition have included such stochastic queries as:

'What are five things you like about Gruyere cheese?'

'Which nightclubs do you go to?'

'Are you allergic to feathers?'

Every time I tried to ask her why she needed to know the answers to these increasingly bizarre and personal questions, or why she was asking me about gruyere cheese at eleven o'clock at night, Kathleen Nolan would deploy one of her two patented distraction techniques. Either she would flat out ignore the question and begin talking a mile a minute in a desperate attempt to confuse and disorient me, or...

"Sweetheart, I'm your mother! I'm not asking for much. After *all* I've done for you over the years, the least you could do is answer a few simple questions! It's not like I'm asking you to give up any state secrets, now am I? Just answer me!"

"But why?" I asked, as I blearily rubbed my eyes and tried to see what time it was on my phone, "Why do you want to know this and why are you calling me in the middle of the night?"

"It's six-thirty, Charlie."

"They do a six-thirty in the morning now? What the hell is that about?"

"Don't be silly, sweetheart. Now answer the question, please."

I groaned loudly. Why was she doing this to me on a Sunday morning? The one day of the week I get to relax and sleep in and my mother is pulling this crap.

Liam, my partner, was still fast asleep beside me. I envied his ability to sleep through just about anything. Although I was seriously tempted to poke him sharply in the side to wake him up. If I had to suffer through this pointless drivel, then so should he. After all, that's what love is all about, isn't it? But ultimately, my kindly, generous nature won out and I left him to his peaceful slumber while I dealt with the mad woman.

"Charlie!" Mum squawked, snapping me back to reality.

"What?"

"I asked you a question!" Mum was starting to lose patience with me.

"Yes, I have a fear of heights! There, are you happy?" I snapped.

"Is it a bad fear of heights? Are you okay on balconies? Would you freak out if you were, say, in a hot air balloon?" Mum queried, sounding like she was writing down my responses.

"That's an oddly specific question. What the hell is all this about, Mum? Seriously, the sun isn't even up!"

"Oh, I'm very sorry to have disturbed you," Mum said, her voice dripping with sarcasm, "I didn't think you'd be so upset with me asking a few simple questions. Especially after I spent ninety-seven hours in labour with you."

"Guilt? Seriously? It's too early in the morning for this bullshit!" I grumbled, pulling the blankets back over my head.

"NINETY SEVEN HOURS!"

"Every time you bring up my birth, you add an extra ten hours to your labour time. It's getting ridiculous."

"You want ridiculous? My pelvis was ridiculous! It was never the same after I gave birth to you and that huge head of yours!"

"I'm sorry, Mother." I said with faux sweetness, "I promise it'll never happen again."

Mum groaned with frustration, clearly annoyed that her attempts to guilt me into submission were failing miserably.

"I'm hanging up now, Mum."

"Wait! One last question..."

Oh god, what now? I was going to need some seriously strong coffee if I was going to get through this conversation without it escalating into matricide. I flung back the blankets and made my way to the kitchen in search of caffeine.

"I need to know if you've set a date for the wedding, Charlie," Mum asked, and her tone sounded serious. It stopped me in my tracks.

"No, not yet."

"Why not? It's been a year since you and Liam announced your engagement. Have you made any plans at all?"

"Mum, do we really need to talk about this right this second?"

"Yes, sweetheart. We do. What's going on? Why aren't you planning the wedding? You aren't having second thoughts, are you?" Mum sounded genuinely panicked.

"No, of course not. Nothing like that," I started the coffee machine and watched as that glorious dark liquid filled my favourite mug, "I promise everything is fine."

"Then what's the problem?"

Honestly, there wasn't a problem. Liam and I were doing great. We were happier and more in love than we had ever been. We had announced our engagement at Christmas last year and we'd both been super excited about the idea of getting married. We still were.

It's just... life got in the way.

I took a sip of my coffee and quietly sighed with satisfaction as the caffeine flowed into me.

"We've both just been really busy recently. We both work long hours and, frankly, wedding planning takes a lot of time. The last thing I want to do at the end of a long workday is sit around picking out floral arrangements or interviewing wedding coordinators. But we'll get around to it. There's no rush. I promise Mum, we'll get there eventually."

Mum seemed to have gone very quiet. I checked the phone to make sure the call hadn't accidentally dropped, but it was still connected.

"Okay then. I leave you to your coffee. Don't forget, Christmas is just around the corner. See you then. Bye, sweetheart!" Mum said, sounding oddly perky. And with that, she ended the call.

Okay, that was weird. Even for Mum. What the hell was all that about?'

"Was that your Mum again?" Liam said, looking sleepy but sexy as he slowly padded his way into the kitchen.

"Yeah, sorry. Did I wake you? She was doing the Spanish Inquisition thing again."

"Nobody expects the Spanish Inquisition!" Liam said as he pulled me into a hug and kissed me swiftly. I chuckled then turned to make him a cup of coffee as he sat down at the kitchen table.

"Your Mum rang me yesterday and started asking me about hot air balloons or something. When I asked why she was asking me about this, she changed the subject and then tried to guilt trip me by telling me about how she was in labour with you for eighty-seven hours. I wasn't really sure what to do with that information."

"I think she's lost her mind. I'm thinking of having her committed." I said as I handed him his mug of steaming coffee.

"Perhaps we should get her a straight jacket for Christmas?" Liam said with a smirk.

"Ugh, please, don't mention the dreaded C word! I'm still trying to come up with a plausible excuse to get us out of it this year. I'm thinking about us contracting some rare, exotic tropical disease like dengue fever or the ebola virus."

"Give it up, Charlie. Like death and taxes, there's just no escaping Christmas with your family."

I groaned dramatically and fell into my chair at the kitchen table, sulking like a toddler. I pouted and made my eyes as big as I could, but Liam was apparently immune to all my tricks. Bugger.

"Fine. But I'm holding you entirely responsible for whatever disaster befalls us as a result."

"Yes, dear," Liam said, sipping his coffee and smiling.

Chapter One – Ho Oh No!

December 23rd – Christmas Eve Eve

"DO WE REALLY have to go?" I asked Liam, trying and failing to keep the whininess out of my voice. It had to be obvious to him that I was stalling for time by pretending to pack up my toiletries in our ensuite bathroom. In reality, I was sitting on the edge of the bathtub and praying for some form of divine intervention that would conveniently prevent us from going to my parent's house for Christmas.

"Time to be a grown-up, Charlie," Liam said through the locked bathroom door and, although I couldn't see his face, I could clearly hear the smirk in his voice.

"I'm a grown-up!" I called out indignantly, "Just last week, I bought a vegetable!"

"Oh, well then, I stand corrected," Liam remarked dryly, "Now unlock this door. I need to pack my shaving things."

Unlike me, Liam didn't have to contend with his family at Christmas. He didn't have to deal with his family at all since they disowned him years earlier. His parents had turned their backs on him after it became apparent that the snooty pair of social-climbing arseholes were more interested in how they appeared in the Melbourne society pages than helping their troubled eldest son, Rory. They made no attempt to help locate him when he went missing while living on the streets. They didn't even acknowledge Rory's death by drug overdose, lest it make them look bad in the eyes of their stuck-up socialite friends.

Liam walked away from his parents after they refused to even attend their own son's funeral. All the while, his extended family chose sides in the fight – with none ultimately choosing Liam's. His relatives were smart enough to know that getting on the bad side of his rich parents would definitely be detrimental to their own social standing. Liam had been hurt by this appalling betrayal, but time and the fact my own demented family had almost immediately adopted him when he had reentered my life two years ago had gone a long way to healing those old wounds.

I sighed, stood up and unlocked the bathroom door, inwardly cursing myself for having failed in my task of coming up with a fool-proof plan to avoid yet another chaotic Christmas with my family. As much as I loved them, the Nolan family had the worst track record when it came to Yuletide festivities. I was also a little concerned that this year's shindig was sizing up to be a whopper when it came to drama if last year's series of holiday debacles were anything to go by.

It had all started out perfectly calm and friendly when Liam and I arrived and announced our engagement. But things quickly began to go south when my parent's special 'dairy-free' cocktail (made especially to accommodate Liam's lactose intolerance) ended up giving everyone a mild case of food poisoning. It turned out that one of the drastically reduced bottles of liqueur my Dad had purchased to make the heinous cocktails had ended up not only being expired but borderline rancid. In hindsight, we should have taken that as an omen of things to come.

Things did perk up briefly though (after the vomiting had subsided, of course) when the classic family card game Uno was randomly selected for Games Night. I briefly thought that Mum had, for once, managed to pick a game that was unlikely to explode into an orgy of violence and hurt feelings. But the aftereffects of the rancid cocktail must have been clouding my judgement.

Events quickly spiralled out of control just one hour into play when Mum got hit with a homemade 'Draw 24' card by Aunt Joss, triggering accusations of cheating and provoking a full-on violent brawl between the two sisters. Once the card game and the punch-up were over, the night ended with a no-score draw.

But the ultimate highlight (or lowlight, depending on your perspective) of last year's Christmas celebrations had to be when Aunt Joss's nicotine patch accidentally fell off and landed in the gravy boat

– right in the middle of Christmas lunch. This not only caused embarrassment for Aunt Joss, but everyone else missing out on the gravy. Mum promptly lost her shit, accusing her sister of deliberately trying to ruin Christmas as payback for the great Uno fight. Joss denied everything, leading Mum to attempt to drown her sister in the ruined gravy. Joss ended up winning the fight when she brained Mum in the head with a small ornamental pumpkin from the table centrepiece.

As usual, we all agreed never to discuss any of this ever again because... *'It's Christmas!'*

And so I dragged myself into gear, grabbed my suitcase and loaded it into the back of the car along with Liam's bags and our Christmas presents for my family. I'd spent way too many hours wrapping crappy gifts in needlessly expensive wrapping paper to forget about them now.

As Liam drove and I gazed at the city as it whizzed by on our way out to the Mornington Peninsula, I couldn't help feeling something was off.

"You always say that." Liam chuckled when I shared my feelings of impending doom. But it was more than the usual apprehension that comes with your standard Nolan family Christmas. Something about this year just felt... off. More off than usual.

Aside from Mum's bizarre series of questions, which I had yet to receive an adequate explanation for, the woman herself had been oddly quiet since our last phone call back in late November. Usually, in the lead-up to Christmas, Kathleen Nolan would be getting frantic and evermore unstable heading toward the big day. But aside from a couple of text messages confirming our attendance, Mum had been effectively incommunicado.

And she wasn't the only one. Ahead of the big day, I would normally be fielding calls and messages from both my siblings regarding the dreaded upcoming events. Yet this year, both Charmaine and Craig had been oddly silent.

Even Bree, my best friend and Craig's girlfriend had apparently found herself out of communication range. At first, I thought I was just being paranoid. Ever since I was promoted a few months ago, Bree and I no longer worked in the same department. We still worked in the same office building, but we simply didn't get to see each other as regularly as we once had. This hadn't affected our friendship too much at first, since we simply made time outside of work hours to catch up for coffee, drinks or dinner when we were both free.

But recently, Bree had been finding it increasingly difficult to find time to meet up. At first, her excuses were perfectly plausible. We both lead busy lives, so it was understandable if she wasn't always available. But soon her reasons for cancelling plans became strange, as if she was making up her excuses on the spot.

My dear friend Bree was a talented woman with many sought-after skills, but lying was most certainly not one of them. When she told me she couldn't make it to a late-night movie because she was having an emergency pap smear, I knew she was avoiding me. When I tried to question her about it, Bree became evasive, started nervously giggling then hung up claiming to be driving through a tunnel.

And through all of it, it hadn't escaped my attention that this series of increasingly peculiar events – Mum's random questions, my siblings going quiet on me and Bree avoiding me like the plague – had all started at approximately the same time. Clearly, something was going on, thus my predictions of impending doom. After all, it's a Nolan family Christmas. This rarely led to glad tidings of joy. Ho Ho Ho? More like Ho Oh No!

Pulling up to my parent's beautiful beachside home, nothing appeared to be especially out of place. My Dad was up on a step ladder as usual, installing his annual Christmas light monstrosity... um, I mean... display on the roof. The front lawn was liberally adorned with empty beer cans from where Dad had discarded them while working on the roof decorations. Everything seemed normal. If 'normal' could ever be used to describe anything related to the Nolan family.

"Hi, Dad!" I called out when I got out of the car, "Merry Christmas Eve Eve!"

"Welcome home, boys!" Dad said without turning around or even looking at down at us, his voice strangely loud. It was almost as if he was trying to announce to the whole street that we had arrived, "I didn't think you'd be here so soon."

I looked toward Liam, who just shrugged at me. Perhaps Dad was losing his hearing? I know Grandma Flo had a tendency to shout whenever she forgot to wear her hearing aids.

"The traffic was good, so we weren't delayed!" I shouted back at him. Dad looked down at me, looking genuinely puzzled.

"Why are you yelling at me?" Dad said, this time speaking at his normal volume.

"You were yelling at us."

"I don't know what you're talking about, Charlie. Perhaps you've had too much to drink."

"Says the man up a step ladder, surrounded by empty beer cans," I said, rolling my eyes.

Any further conversation was brought to a screeching halt by a commotion at the front door. My mother came flying out of the house looking very flustered. She was wearing a red floral silk dressing gown, her hair was pulled up as if she was caught in the middle of styling it and, most curiously of all, she was wearing a pink feather boa around her neck. She looked like a narcoleptic drag queen who was running late for a show.

"Boys!" Mum said with a voice that came close to manic, sporting a smile that was equally as frenzied, "We weren't expecting you so soon!"

"Apparently. Did we catch you in the middle of your afternoon delight with your boyfriend?" I chucked, trying not to full-on guffaw at the look of indignation on my mother's face at such an outrageous suggestion. Liam shook his head at me, but couldn't help but smile too.

"You better not be!" My father grumbled from the roof, "I should be all the boyfriend you ever need, woman!"

"Oh, you are, you big ol' hunk of man-meat, you!" Mum called out to her husband, giggling like a schoolgirl and swinging her boa like a stripper.

"And don't you forget it!" Dad growled playfully.

Mum blushed furiously, fanning herself as if my father's caveman posturing had her all overcome with teenage levels of hormones.

"Gross," I grumbled to myself.

I was no longer laughing. Teasing my Mum was fun. Watching my parents flirt outrageously in front of me was not. It was also way outside the realms of normal behaviour for a Nolan Family Christmas. Something was definitely going on.

"So..." I said, desperately trying to change the subject to literally anything, "We'd better get our stuff inside and up to our room." I gestured to the back of the car where our luggage was stowed. It was then I heard a quiet cough from behind the closed front door. Mum's eye twitched ever so slightly.

"Not until I've had a big hug from both of you. I'm so glad to see you both!" Mum said as she grabbed me in a bone-crushing hug that would be ruled an illegal action in even the most brutal of death sports. She eventually released me after what felt like an inordinately long time, but only after I complained that I was having trouble breathing. Mum immediately threw herself into Liam's arms and began squeezing the life out of him too.

I took this opportunity to grab some of the luggage out of the car and head towards the house. This action did not go unnoticed by my father.

"Kathleen!" Dad called out.

My mother quickly released Liam and dashed over to me, blocking my entry.

"Watch out, Mum. These things are heavy."

"You can't go in there!" Mum said, her manic smile now looking more panic-stricken.

"Why not?" Liam said, arms filled with our Christmas presents.

"It's... um... bad luck!" Mum said.

"Bad luck?" I asked, wondering what the hell was going on.

"Yes! I... um... spilled some salt earlier! Yes! And I forgot to toss some over my shoulder for good luck. So if you go inside, the house might fall down on you or something. We can't have that, can we? It's Christmas, after all!" Mum babbled.

Well, this was a completely normal thought process to have and not at all completely insane. It was clear my mother had finally gone totally bonkers. Either that, or she'd accidentally sprinkled some methamphetamines on her cornflakes that morning.

"Mum, have you been inhaling your hairspray again?"

Mum's only response was to laugh maniacally in a way that made her seem even more unhinged. I slowly took a step back, accidentally backing into Liam.

It was then the front door burst open and my little sister Charmaine and her partner Robyn smiled wide at us. There was a twinkle in their eyes that immediately put me on edge.

"It's okay, Mum! I... um... cleaned up all the salt. They can come in now." Charmaine said, standing aside and ushering Liam and I inside. I ended up dumping the luggage in the living room rather than trying to carry it all the way upstairs to our room. After carrying the heavy bags for so long outside, I decided to take a break rather than start the Yuletide season with a herniated spinal disc.

Mum leapt ahead of us and gave us big kisses and more hugs. Thankfully this time, no bones were broken.

"I have a surprise for you boys!" Mum singsonged to us in a way that made her sound like a demon-possessed doll from a horror movie. I looked over at Liam and, once again, he shrugged.

Mum suddenly snatched our hands and proceeded to drag us to the back of the house, toward the patio area. She quickly shoved us out the back door and we were confronted by something I had not been expecting.

The patio area had been completely transformed. Gone was the usual backyard barbecue and tinsel hanging from the covered entertaining deck. In its place was a bright, elegant space with everything swaddled in white. But not a Christmas white. Not a snowy, wintery white. This was fancy tulle and classy white linen. Strings of white twinkle lights hanging from the rafters. The long dining table was set with the best china and glassware.

When I looked up and saw the large printed banner hanging from the patio roof, my whole brain misfired and my heart stopped. In large, bold silver letters, the banner read 'HAPPY BACHELOR PARTY CHARLIE + LIAM!'

Oh my god...

Chapter Two – Surprises and Betrayals

"SURPRISE!" MY MOTHER cried out with ardent enthusiasm, in spite of the fact that nobody else joined in on her ebullient pronouncement. The silence that followed was slightly awkward, especially when Mum started clapping. Nobody joined in on that either.

"Um, Mum?" Charmaine blatantly stage-whispered, much to her girlfriend's amusement, "You have to tell people beforehand if you want them to shout out 'Surprise' too, otherwise nothing will happen. Also, you have to gather everyone together in the same place at the same time. Stuff like that doesn't just happen spontaneously."

Mum stopped clapping and visibly deflated. However, she quickly recovered enough to turn to Liam and I. Her smile was so wide and unnatural, she looked like she'd fallen asleep with a coathanger in her mouth.

"Well, boys! What do you think?" Mum said, waving her hands around to draw our attention to... well... everything. Liam seemed to be at a loss for words and looked to me for direction.

"I'm not exactly sure what to think. What's going on, Mum?" I said carefully, trying hard not to offend my mother, as she appeared to be on the edge of some sort of party-induced hysteria. Unexpectedly, she seemed surprised by my question.

"What do you think is going on?"

"Well, you seem to have made some pretty radical changes to Christmas this year." I offered mildly, trying to distract myself from the minor panic attack that was currently boiling up inside me. Looking at the banner hanging above us, it was clear what Mum had planned. But I didn't think my brain was quite ready to comprehend the enormity of it all just yet. Considering what normally results when my mother plans a Christmas party, I could only imagine the horrors that would be unleashed if she...

"Charlie, are you okay?" Liam said, breaking me from my internal reverie, looking concerned, "You've gone very pale."

"And his eyes are so wide!" Robyn said.

"He looks like one of those bunnies you see on the road at night. Just frozen in place, terrified of the cars on the highway. Right before they get squished by a truck!" Charmaine said, grinning evilly.

"It's not just Christmas, sweetheart!" Mum said, completely ignoring everyone's comments, "Welcome to your surprise wedding!"

It was lucky we were standing outside. If we had been inside, I'm, pretty sure my uncontrolled gasp would have sucked every last ounce of oxygen from the house.

"Wow!" Liam said, slightly too enthusiastically while taking me in his arms, "That's amazing Kathleen. Thank you so much! Charlie, isn't this amazing?"

"Are you out of your fucking mind?" I whispered to him, still trying not to have a complete nervous breakdown, "Do you have any idea how supremely bad an idea this is?"

"You don't want to marry me?" Liam asked, his voice quiet, and I suddenly felt like a prick.

"Of course I want to marry you. But this is Kathleen Nolan we're talking about here. Inventor of ye olde Yuletide street riot!"

Liam chuckled, presumably reassured, but I was still more than a little disturbed that the woman who could turn a minor incident with a gravy boat into an explosive orgy of aggression and violence, had apparently taken on the responsibility of organising what was supposed be the happiest day of my life. I visibly shuddered.

"You don't have anything to worry about, sweetheart." Mum said with her usual misplaced confidence, "I've taken care of everything. All you two have to do is show up and get married. Everything else has been organised. Nothing can possibly go wrong!"

Famous last words. I quickly moved three paces away from my mother, in hopes that the lightning bolt wouldn't hit me too.

"I'm not sure how reassuring that is," I said, looking to the sky nervously, "given that the 'surprise' part of this event has already gone tits up." I pointed out. Mum was undaunted.

"Charlie! Watch your language!" My father bellowed from the roof. I swear that man has hearing like a bat.

"Well, something always goes wrong when you're planning a major event like a wedding," Mum said confidently, "Better to get it over and done with now, don't you think?"

So speaks the woman who's Christmas parties usually end in either bedlam erupting or a group trip to the nearest emergency room.

"I think I need a drink," I say wearily and Liam escorted me to the kitchen, with everyone following close behind.

"That's the spirit, sweetheart!" Mum cheered, clearly missing that I wasn't looking to celebrate.

When I got to the kitchen, I found my Aunt Joss sitting at the table arranging flowers into large centrepieces. She was drinking white wine out of a large plastic tumbler and humming merrily to herself. I grabbed the open wine bottle and poured myself a glass too. Wandering over to the window, I looked out on the backyard and nearly choked on my mouthful of wine at the sight of my uncle.

Now, my Uncle Jack had always been fond of festive costumes. Every year, much to his wife's chagrin and embarrassment, he would don a dizzying array of outfits ranging from classic holiday characters to abstract artistic projects that had clearly been custom-designed to my uncle's exacting specifications. But nothing could have prepared me for the sight of Uncle Jack prancing around the backyard dressed in a disturbingly skimpy cherub outfit. He was apparently practicing scattering rose petals, as the back lawn was covered in a floral blanket of blush pink.

"Is Uncle Jack dressed as Cupid?" I gasped in mild horror.

"No," Aunt Joss grumbled through gritted teeth, "According to him, he's dressed as 'Eros' and yes, there *is* a difference, apparently," she rolled her eyes and knocked back the rest of her wine, clearly having had this exact conversation several times already.

"Why is he dressed as Eros?" Liam asked, mesmerised at the vision of Uncle Jack skipping barefoot around the clothesline, his bare chest and belly jiggling with every bound.

" He's your flower girl!" Mum said with disturbing enthusiasm.

"Call him whatever you want," Joss said snatching the wine bottle back from me and refilling her cup and taking a huge swig, "I call it my husband dancing around in a tutu, flashing his man-boobs at everyone. Merry fucking Christmas!"

"Actually, Robyn was going to be the flower girl," Mum said quietly, sounding mildly perturbed, "But Jack insisted he would look better in the costume. He's been out there practicing for hours. The backyard looks like there was a terrorist attack at the Chelsea Flower Show."

Mum opened the kitchen window and stuck her head out, "Jack! You better gather up all those bloody rose petals. If you waste them all before the big day – I will destroy you!" she said in a tone of voice that brooked absolutely no argument. Uncle Jack blanched and immediately got down on his hands and knees to start picking up the petals. It was a shame he had apparently forgotten to put on underwear beneath his skimpy costume. My retinas didn't need that disturbing visual.

"Mum, why didn't you tell us about this beforehand? Don't you think Liam and I should have been involved in the planning of our own wedding?" I asked, as my mother randomly started wiping down the perfectly spotless surfaces of the kitchen, possibly to metaphorically wipe away the image of her brother-in-law's anus.

"You've had a year to plan it and so far you haven't done a single thing. And besides, it wouldn't have been much of a surprise if I told you about it, now would it, darling!"

She had me there. How was this my life?

"But how are we going to organise the guest list at such short notice? You can't just invite people to a wedding at Christmas on a couple of days notice!"

"Oh, sweetheart!" Mum said, as if I were some sort of simpleton, "That's all been taken care of!"

But how could it have 'all been taken care of?' How would Mum know who to invite or even how to contact them? The only way she could do that would be if...

I slowly turned to Liam, who was now staring at the floor and looking very guilty.

"You knew about this, didn't you?" I accused. Liam blushed, then smiled his awkward smile that always made my heart melt.

"I thought it would be fun."

"Betrayer!" I hissed. He must have known about all this for ages and never said a word.

"Your Mum swore me to secrecy!" Liam blurted out. I tried not to laugh at how quickly he had ratted out my mother. I turned my scowl on her.

"Double Betrayer!" I hissed, but Mum wasn't even remotely phased.

"Oh, darling! I've always dreamed of throwing a gay wedding! And since your sister 'doesn't believe in marriage,'" Mum said with barely disguised acid, "I won't be missing out on my son's gay wedding!"

I shook my head, "Can't it just be a wedding? Why does it have to be a 'gay' wedding?"

"Yuk!" My mother said, looking like she might actually be physically sick, "Straight weddings are so last century! Embrace your identity, Charlie. You're here! You're queer! Get used to it!"

Liam gave me a hug. Mum swooned at the romance of it all. Joss helped herself to another bottle of wine and I tried not to die inside. This was going to be a Nolan Family Christmas for the record books.

~

"Did you know about this?" I confronted my best friend, Bree, the moment she arrived with my brother. Craig, the battle-hardened former soldier and now Bree's boyfriend, knew a skirmish was incoming and wisely dashed upstairs with their luggage while I engaged the enemy. Bree didn't seem even slightly intimidated.

"Your mum promised I could be the flower girl!" she said triumphantly, revelling openly in her disgusting treachery.

"I thought thirty pieces of silver was the going rate." I muttered under my breath. Bree slapped my shoulder playfully.

"Stop pouting. Try and think about things from my perspective. I never got to be a flower girl when I was growing up. Now, I get to be a pretty little girl, scattering rose petals and wearing a metric fuckton of tulle!"

"I wouldn't be so sure. Mum double-crossed you. Uncle Jack is the new flower girl."

"Like hell he is!" Bree's scowled, "This is my moment. I'm not letting some weirdo in a penguin suit take away my special day! I'll dance on your mother's grave!"

"Um, you do know it's *my* special day, right?" I asked gently, concerned that my friend had somehow become a bridezilla despite not actually being the bride.

"It's not always about you, Charlie!" she quietly seethed.

"Don't worry," I soothed, "Mum appears to have bought about seven thousand tonnes of rose petals. I'm sure there will be plenty for both of you to scatter. Meanwhile, how the hell could you not tell me about any of this?"

Bree sniffed, clearly still aggrieved at being usurped by my uncle, "Your Mum swore me to secrecy. Plus the flower girl thing sealed the deal. But mostly, your family gatherings are always a hoot. I wanted to be on the ground floor for this psycho drama!"

"I will never forgive you for this." I said, with absolutely no heat.

"Yeah, you will. Just you wait until you see what's coming up!"

"You know whats going to happen? Tell me! Tell me everything!"

"Nuh uh. It's a surprise! Your mum threatened me with death."

"You could take her. I have confidence in your killing skills."

"That's very true. But I want to see how this plays out."

I narrowed my eyes at Bree. For her betrayal and her unwillingness to rat out my Mum's evil plans, my dear best friend needed to be punished.

"Mum?" I called out, "Bree says she wants you to plan *her* wedding too!"

Bree froze, her eyes going as wide as saucers. I smirked wickedly at her. Mum came flying out of the kitchen and embraced Bree in a bone-crushing, crash-tackle bear hug while congratulating her on her supposed engagement. If looks could kill, the one Bree shot my way would have reduced me to a pile of radioactive dust. I simply blew her a kiss and walked away chuckling.

Let's see how *that* plays out...

Chapter Three – Suite Confessions

LIAM AND I were soon ushered, rather forcefully, upstairs to what my mother disturbingly referred to as the 'bachelor suite.' In reality, it was my parent's bedroom.

"Why are you putting us in here? What's wrong with my old bedroom?" I asked, puzzled at this unscheduled change of accommodations.

"Sweetheart, I have to finish setting up for the party tonight. I don't want you looking out your bedroom window and spoiling the surprises!" Mum said with a giddy grin.

Before I could tell her that any more surprises may just prove to be fatal, for her as well as me, Mum had closed the door and dashed away downstairs, effectively ending our conversation.

I turned my attention to Liam, who was sitting on my parent's king size bed with his best million megawatt smile. The same smile that usually made me weak at the knees and melted me into a puddle. Usually. But I knew this smile was being deployed as a distraction. He knew he was in for it.

"You can knock it off. That smile won't make me forget that you're a vile, evil betrayer!" I said dramatically, scowling at him to punctuate my displeasure. Liam simply turned his smile up a few more megawatts, the bastard, and I felt a few butterflies attempting to flutter around inside me. I did my level best to squash them down. "How could you not warn me about this?"

"I just thought it would be nice. Besides, we're going to get married anyway. At least this way, we won't have to deal with the stress of organising everything." Liam said.

"No, we'll just get to deal with the stress of whatever the hell my mother has planned!"

"It's a wedding. How bad could it be?"

"How bad could it be? Seriously? A wedding organised by the woman who could turn a game of Scrabble in to a bare-knuckle boxing match over a triple word score and the use of a letter Q?"

This seemed to give Liam pause. He had apparently forgotten, or possibly repressed, the great Scrabble incident from last Christmas. After Tiddlywinks had proven far too spicy for our family, Mum had attempted to cool things down by switching us over to something a little less provocative. Believing a simple word game was unlikely to lead to any explosive fights or emotional meltdowns, Mum had pulled out the old Scrabble board and doubtlessly congratulated herself internally on how easily disaster had been averted.

Oh, how very wrong she was.

Everything had been going swimmingly until Liam played the word 'Qi' – a perfectly legitimate but obscure word that managed to turn the tide in the game, netting him a game-winning score and leaving my Mum in the dust. Mum, having enjoyed one too many Christmas cocktails, had lost her temper, flipped the Scrabble board over and 'accidentally' toppled the coffee table over with it.

The ensuing commotion had inadvertently startled Uncle Perry, who had been peacefully dozing in a nearby armchair, who then threw his hands up in shock – accidentally socking Mum right in the face. Before anyone knew what was happening, Dad and his brother were on their feet and punching each other right there in the middle of the living room. The two men ended up spending the new year with swollen eye sockets and split lips. Mum's black eye had been epic. Liam had wished he'd just skipped his turn.

"I hadn't thought of that. But I'm sure it'll be fine." he said.

"Famous last words." I muttered.

"It'll be great, just you wait and see. We'll get married, your family will be happy, we'll be happy. And then... we'll get to have the wedding night," he wiggled his eyebrows suggestively, "and we can maybe do that thing you like..." he said huskily.

My brain short-circuited. I knew exactly what he was talking about. While we weren't the kinkiest couple in the world, there was one thing I liked that wasn't exactly vanilla.

"Does that mean you brought the...?" I asked, shyly.

"Oh yes," Liam said, smugly, "Both sizes."

I quivered and blushed brightly. Liam chuckled, his eyes twinkling. I suddenly realised he was distracting me again.

"Okay, spill it! Everything you know. What's that lunatic woman planned?"

Liam sighed, clearly giving up on any attempt to distract me further. "Honestly, I don't really know anything. Your mum wouldn't give me any specifics. She just kept saying it was a surprise. I thought it sounded kind of nice."

"Nice?!" I exclaimed, but my incredulity melted away at the slightly sad look on Liam's face.

"Yeah, it's nice to have parents who care about you that much. Who'd plan a wedding for you. Who want to be a part of the biggest day of your life."

I immediately felt like a piece of shit. From Liam's perspective, my family, in spite of it's eccentricities, must seem like a dream come true compared to his.

I pulled him into my arms and held him tight. "I'm sorry. I don't mean to sound ungrateful about it all. It's just my family are..."

"Totally insane?" Liam suggested with a soft chuckle. I nodded into his neck and smiled.

"Plus, I find the idea of releasing control of the biggest day of my life into the hands of my mother to be, well, terrifying."

"I'm sure it will all be lovely in the end."

While I had my doubts about that, I decided to adopt a positive attitude. I loved my family, lunatics that they were, and they loved me. I was sure it would all be fine.

It would *NOT* all be fine.

Chapter Four – What's In The Bag?

AFTER AN HOUR of waiting in my parent's bedroom, I was starting to get frustrated and bored. I'd tried to pass the time by snooping through my parent's stuff, but aside from finding my Dad's secret stash of chocolate Wagon Wheel biscuits, which Mum had officially banned from the house ever since her weird dieting phase back in the early 90s, their possessions were disappointingly dull.

Liam had distracted himself by diving into Mum's battered old paperback copy of *Fetish* by Tara Moss while occasionally shooting disapproving looks in my direction as I mindlessly rummaged through my parent's walk-in wardrobe. I was undeterred by this. If my parents wanted to trap me up here for goodness knows how long, they had to expect me to ransack their bedroom and dig out all their dirty little hidden secrets.

Although, to be honest, a bag of Wagon Wheels stuffed in an old gym bag and Mum's collection of ancient Avon lipsticks were not exactly going to light up the local gossip pages. I tried not to pout as I gave up on snooping.

Eventually my patience was exhausted. I was not going to sit up here forever. I needed to know what the hell was going on downstairs. It was time for me to stage a jailbreak. I quietly and sneakily crept over to the bedroom door while Liam shook his head and continued to read. I carefully gripped the doorknob and gave it a gentle twist.

I pulled the door open ever so slightly – just enough so I could take a quick unobserved peek outside. Admittedly, the chances of me discovering anything earth-shattering in the upstairs hallway, miles away from the action out in the backyard, was remote. But after an hour or so stuck in my parent's bedroom, I was starved for entertainment. I cracked the door open a little more, but as soon as I did, a loud whistling noise split the air. Robyn, my sister's girlfriend, had been surreptitiously standing guard close by and had sounded the alarm at my attempted escape. I quickly slammed the door shut and dashed over to Liam on the bed, who dropped his book and looked up with wide eyes as the bedroom door flew open and banged against the wall. In strode a scowling Charmaine, followed close behind by a smiling Robyn. Robyn, sweet as she was, seemed to be enjoying this whole situation far too much for my liking.

"And where do you think you're going?" Charmaine asked accusingly, her arms crossed in a gesture that showed she meant business.

"Gee, I dunno, Warden. How about anywhere I damn well please?" I said, standing up straight and crossing my own arms. For some reason, I didn't look nearly as tough as Charmaine did. "For crying out loud, Sis, How much longer do we have to stay up here? This is getting ridiculous!"

Charmaine, to her credit, made a valiant attempt to maintain her tough-guy scowl, but even she had to realise this whole situation went beyond Mum's usual level of psychotic behaviour.

"Now you understand why *we* never want to get married." Charmaine said with an evil smirk, "But you can relax, it'll all be over soon."

That didn't sound ominous at all. Charmaine turned and took a large paper bag from her still smiling girlfriend, then faced Liam and I, holding the bag outstretched to us.

"What's this? Rations?" I asked, gently shaking the bag. Liam looked at it equally curiously.

"Costumes. By order of Her Majesty downstairs!" Robyn replied with a girlish giggle.

"Costumes?" Liam asked, suddenly sounding nervous. His reaction was the first indicator to me that he was indeed telling the truth when he said he didn't know what my mother had planned for us.

"Oh, don't worry," I patted Liam's arm, "Remember what you said earlier, *'I'm sure it will all be lovely in the end!'*" I said, mockingly, using Liam's own words against him. For the first time, Liam looked a hell of a lot less confident about this whole situation.

"Well, open it up, Charlie." Liam sighed with resignation. Charmaine and Robyn were practically vibrating with excitement, which only disturbed me more. Clearly, they knew exactly what was in the bag – and their sheer giddiness to see my reaction could only spell doom.

"I can't help but be concerned about any costumes that come supplied in an old paper bag from a butcher's shop. Was it designed by Lady Gaga, by any chance?" I muttered as I opened the bag carefully and peered inside. What I spotted was so disturbing, my brain had difficulty processing the full horror of it all – especially considering that my MOTHER was behind it.

"Absolutely not!" I said with finality, closing the bag and dropping it on the floor with a resounding thud.

The two women laughed hysterically. Liam, having not seen inside the bag of nightmares, was confused but clearly concerned by my reaction.

"You have to!" Charmaine whined, "Mum said so!"

"I don't care! I'm not doing it. It's not happening and nobody can make me!" This whole this was preposterous. My mother had finally crossed the line.

"Mum said," Charmaine said after a moment's silence, "that if you don't wear it, I'm allowed to tell Liam about what you were caught doing in the garden shed on your fifteenth birthday..."

My heart froze. Charmaine's grin was positively evil. Liam's eyebrows rose. Robyn suppressed another giggle. I looked my sister in the eye, blushing so hard my face felt like it was on fire, and fixed her with a withering gaze. Not for the first time in my life, I wished I had the ability to disintegrate people using just the power of my mind. I would have truly enjoyed watching my sister explode into a cloud of microscopic fragments.

"I hate you so much right now." I said through gritted teeth, as I reluctantly stooped down and picked up the paper bag.

"What did you do in the garden shed?" Liam asked with genuine curiosity.

"Well..." Charmaine began.

"Shut up!" I barked, probably a little louder than I had intended, if the startled looks on everyone's faces were anything to go by. Charmaine eventually smirked and grabbed the doorknob.

"You have ten minutes, boys. Get ready for a night you'll never forget!" my bitch of a sister said, cackling maniacally, as she and Robyn exited the room and closed the door behind them. Their retreating footsteps were muffled only by the sound of their uproarious laughter.

"Did you get caught doing something kinky in the garden shed?" Liam asked with an amused smirk.

"Sure, and I used *meatloaf* as my safe word." I said, rolling my eyes.

"I'm almost afraid to ask, but why *meatloaf*?"

"Isn't it obvious? Because I would do anything for love, but I won't do that."

Liam just shook his head at me. I hoped that would put an end to his questions regarding this subject, but I knew deep down Liam wasn't as easily distracted as me.

I picked up the paper bag, took it over to the bed. I opened it up, turned it over and spilled it's contents over Mum's gaudy floral bedspread. Liam looked at the assemblage of disturbing items and his eyes bulged in disbelief.

"Seriously, what the hell did you do in the garden shed?" he asked again.

"Nothing!" I said, refusing to go anywhere near that Pandora's Box of teenage anxiety, "Just shut up and get dressed." I grumbled as I started to strip off my clothes.

I was going to kill my mother for this.

Chapter Five – Dressed To Distress

WHEN LIAM STEPPED out of the ensuite bathroom, he looked as utterly ridiculous as I did. I noted with some sick amusement that the barely contained grin he had worn when I stepped out of the bathroom only a few minutes earlier had suddenly evaporated. His cocky expression had been replaced with a random collage of embarrassment, confusion and a light smattering of ignominy. It's interesting how things aren't quite so funny when they happen to you.

He stood before me, dressed exactly as I was, wearing an obscenely tight pair of sparkly gold hot pants that even Kylie Minogue would have objected to wearing. His bare torso was slathered in shimmering gold body glitter. The ensemble was completed with a white sash that proclaimed Liam to be the *'Stud King.'*

In normal circumstance, this imagery would have been enough to leave me laughing myself into a fit of uncontrollable nausea, but I couldn't help but question why he got to be the *'Stud King'* while for some reason, my sash declared me to be a *'Slut In Training.'* I was really trying not to read too much into these sashes, or my mother's thought processes behind their selection.

"Okay," Liam said, looking at himself in Mum's full length mirror and shuddering, "Maybe now we should be concerned about what your mother has planned for us."

"*Now* we should be concerned?" I said, making no attempt to hide my incredulity.

"Seriously, what the hell is with these costumes? Does she even know what a wedding is?"

"We're not having a wedding, remember. It's a *gay wedding*. And besides, we're not getting married tonight. This nonsense is apparently for the bachelor party."

Liam looked slightly aghast. "Given that *this* is the dress code for tonight, I'm kinda worried these costumes are just the tip of the iceberg."

I nodded gravely. My partner was finally getting it. And he thought a Nolan Family Christmas was a nightmare. He ain't seen nothing yet.

"Oh, God!" Liam groaned, "She can't be serious about us actually wearing these?"

"Nothing surprises me anymore when it comes to my mother." I said with resignation. "Come on, let's go downstairs and get this over with. The sooner it's done, the sooner we can drink our weight in alcohol and forget whatever the hell is about to happen."

Liam smiled sweetly, kissed me swiftly on the lips, then took my hand and guided me out of the bedroom. In the hall, there was no sign of Charmaine or Robyn, so we made our way down the stairs to the rear of the house. Approaching the back door near the kitchen, loud dance music with a thumping baseline could be heard emanating from the direction of the patio area. I noticed that all the curtains and blinds at the rear of the house were closed, clearly an attempt to hide whatever was going on outside from our prying eyes. Bright, multicoloured disco lights could be seen beaming in around the edges of the window coverings.

I pulled back the heavy curtain covering the rear sliding door and Liam and I stepped out onto the patio. The entire Nolan family was there, including many far flung relatives that were only ever seen for births, deaths or weddings. Everyone was busy eating canapes, drinking and chatting amongst themselves. Nobody had apparently noticed our arrival. I swallowed down my embarrassment at being seen in public wearing such an insane outfit and announced our presence to the crowd.

"Here we are, everyone!" I called out, hoping I would be heard over the music. As one, my family turned toward us. Their faces shifted to expressions of shock and utter dismay. My father's eyes nearly bugged out of his head. My uncle's jaw hit the floor. My Grandmother gave Liam a salacious wink that made me want to slap her. But my mother's expression was the most curious of all. She seemed to be as shocked as everyone else.

"What the hell are you two boys wearing?" Mum cried, looking like she was struggling not to laugh, scream or possibly pass out.

"What do you mean? These stupid costumes were your idea!" I said indignantly.

"My idea? What are you talking about, Charlie?"

That's when I heard the laughter. My sister and her girlfriend cackling uncontrollably like a pair of bog witches while pointing in our direction. I narrowed my eyes at Charmaine and knew we had been had.

"You!" I roared. "What the hell?"

"What?" Charmaine with a shrug, completely unrepentant. "It's traditional to prank the groom at his bachelor party. And luckily for me, I got to do it to two grooms!"

The entire family erupted into fits of laughter. Liam looked embarrassed. I looked murderous. Grandma continued to ogle Liam. I tried to calm myself and regain my composure. Charmaine smirked at me, clearly very proud of herself. That's when a thought occurred to me, and I smirked back at her. My sister knew this smirk. Her expression faltered.

"You know, Sis, you're not the only one who has a few interesting stories from the past to tell. Why don't I tell Robyn all about your holiday to the Gold Coast after you graduated from high school?"

Charmaine's smirk was gone in an instant, replaced with a look of blind panic. She went pale as realisation set in that she had seriously miscalculated when pulling a prank on me.

"Come on, sweetheart! Let's go get ourselves some drinks!" Charmaine said, practically dragging Robyn away with her as she bid a hasty retreat. Robyn squawked indignantly, clearly not happy at missing out on my salacious tale of my sister's disgusting trip to Sea World. I chuckled to myself. I'd catch up with Robyn later. My sister needed to be punished.

"You know, Charlie, after some thought, those costumes are actually quite fitting for a gay bachelor party. I approve." Mum said as she and Dad passed by on their way to the kitchen.

I had hoped Liam and I would have time to go back upstairs and get changed out of these preposterous costumes, but before we could make a break for it, my parents reemerged from the kitchen baring trays of their home made cocktails.

As if tonight wasn't going badly enough.

"What's with your family and weird embarrassing secrets?" Liam asked, "And don't think I've forgotten about that whole garden shed thing. I want answers, mister!"

"Oh, look! Mum and Dad are bringing out cocktails. Let's go have some refreshing, delicious cocktails!" I said in a chirpy tone of voice that sounded maniacal even to my own ears, as I desperately tried to change to subject. No way was I telling Liam about *that* incident.

"Jeez, it must be juicy. You know I'll get it out of you eventually." Liam promised.

"I wouldn't bet on it." I muttered to myself.

Chapter Six – Cocktails and Cock-Ups

KEVIN AND KATHLEEN Nolan's attempts at making cocktails should be outlawed by the United Nation's Geneva Convention as a crime against humanity. Every Christmas, my parents would endeavour to invent some amazing new festive drink to serve to their party guests, and every year their party guests end up with unnaturally-coloured substances being forcibly ejected from every orifice.

Those outside of my family often accuse me of exaggerating my parents holiday antics. But I'm still convinced that, if my parents were ever to fall on hard times and needed to make some quick cash, their 'Nutella Surprise' cocktail from Christmas five years ago could be successfully sold to international terrorist groups as a devastating chemical weapon. I don't care how delicious my mother insisted it was. No drink should make your sweat turn orange.

So when I saw my parents coming over bearing trays of their latest liquid atrocity… I mean… refreshing beverage creation, I knew we were in for a doozy this year. The trays were densely filled with tall glass tumblers filled with a strange, milky blue substance. The cocktail was served over ice and garnished liberally with what appeared to be dead flies, but on closer inspection turned out to be raisins. I looked at Liam, who looked both puzzled and mildly terrified of my parent's latest invention.

"Well, looks like I'll be safe this year," Liam muttered under his breath, "I've never been more thankful to be lactose intolerant."

I just smirked at him. Liam *thought* he was safe. But he had clearly forgotten than ever since he had reentered my life, my parents had bent over backwards to accommodate his digestive issues. I would bet good money that this sin against nature was one hundred percent dairy free just for Liam's benefit.

"Drink up, boys!" my father said boisterously, thrusting his tray in our direction and motioning us to help ourselves.

"What... is it?" I asked carefully, taking one of the glasses and giving it an experimental sniff. The aroma was unusual but not immediately off-putting, which was something of a minor miracle given who made it.

"We call it a *Melted Snowman*" Mum said cheerily, her smile wide as the Sydney Harbour Bridge.

"Yeah, but what's in it?" I pressed.

"It's made with love!" Mum replied in a sweet tone of voice that was both strained and a little disturbing.

Dad moved off and began passing the glasses amongst the rest of the party guests who, despite some initial reservations, started guzzling them down like they would any other alcoholic drink. My family needed to seriously analyse their drinking habits, not to mention their memory problems, given that none of them seem to remember the nightmare cocktails of Christmases gone by.

Liam and I looked at each other, each holding a glass, silently daring each other to take a sip first. Eventually, Liam lost the battle of wills and took a small taste. His expression remained neutral.

"It's... okay, I guess."

High praise indeed. Mum seemed to be satisfied as her manic, Joker-like smile widened even more and she headed off to distribute drinks to the rest of the party.

I watched Liam for a few more seconds. He didn't vomit. He didn't pass out. He didn't go blind. All of these were commendable attributes in any cocktail made by my parents. I sighed and reluctantly took a sip of my cocktail.

The moment that mysterious, light blue liquid touched my tongue, I saw Liam smirk ever so slightly.

Shit.

I can honestly say the *Melted Snowman* was not the worst thing my parents had ever made. But it would comfortably sit somewhere in the top five. It tasted like a grotesque combination of toothpaste and orange liqueur, with just a splash of soy sauce. It took all my discipline to delicately spit the vile liquid back into my glass without causing a scene or allowing my mother to see my obvious displeasure.

"You're a bastard." I said under my breath as Liam chuckled wickedly to himself like some old timey villain who'd just tied me to the railroad tracks.

"If I had to suffer, so did you. Love is about sharing everything with your partner." Liam said.

"I don't remember you being this evil before. I think my family have been a bad influence on you."

Liam shrugged, but continued to giggle evilly to himself. I grabbed both of our glasses and surreptitiously poured their contents into the potted fern next to us. I was disturbed to notice that the hardy plant seemed to visibly wilt within seconds. Abandoning our glasses on the table, I escorted Liam to the other end of the patio to distance us from the now very sickly fern so we could get ourselves some decent drinks.

~

After about an hour, my family as a group had once again demonstrated that their tastebuds were clearly defective. They had somehow managed to polish off the entire supply of *Melted Snowman* cocktails. Liam and I, not being huge drinkers, nursed a couple of glasses of scotch. While the two of us were a little tipsy (most likely due to the tentative sips we took of the cocktail rather than the scotch) the rest of the family were roaring drunk. The backyard was filled with loud, high-spirited laughter, delighted squealing and outrageous behaviour.

Liam and I should probably have gone upstairs and changed out of our ridiculous costumes, but given it was a hot and humid night, neither of us could be bothered. So we sat there, dressed in our matching hot pants and hen's night sashes, watching the lunacy unfold.

Meanwhile, Mum and Dad had disappeared from the patio area and were, most likely, cleaning up in the kitchen or preparing more party snacks. Honestly, they could have been throwing darts at each other's heads, and it would have been a more relaxing night than Mum's sister was having.

Aunt Joss was chasing a very drunk Uncle Jack around the backyard, desperately trying to get him to cover up. Jack's quiver had snapped off and his skimpy shorts had split up the back, giving everyone a disturbing and very much unwanted view of what Jack insisted on calling his 'chocolate starfish.' Joss begged him to put on some clothes.

"Eros should be allowed to show off his love hole!" Jack cackled as he drunkenly shed the shredded shorts altogether and began streaking across the lawn. My family cheered and howled like wolves at the 'full moon' on display. Aunt Joss looked mortified. But she needn't have worried. Her husband wasn't the only one getting drunk and naked.

Uncle Perry and his son, Josh, were apparently having some kind of impromptu drunken bodybuilding contest. While my younger cousin was a junior bodybuilder and has the physique for such a competition, the same could not be said for his father.

Perry, who never met a pie he didn't adore, had stripped down to his underwear and was posing himself in increasingly silly ways while his abundant belly jiggled with each movement. To be fair, Josh wasn't performing at his best either, given that both men had clearly had more than a few cocktails and were now having trouble standing. The result was two very drunk men in their underwear, leaning against a pole while desperately trying to flex their arms, legs and possibly earlobes. My grandmother found the whole scene hilarious and began throwing coins at the two men while cackling wildly and shouting "Take it off! Take it off!"

Grandma Flo was back to her old tricks after a brief hiatus. For a long time, my grandmother had been known for her veracious appetite for younger men, much to my mother's chagrin. But after an – ahem – unfortunate incident a couple of Christmases ago, Flo decided to try dating men her own age. Unfortunately, after she accidentally broke one of her boyfriend's hips during an event she refused to discuss in any real detail, she decided to go back to her toy boys. This year's arm candy looked like something out of an Avril Lavigne music video. When I first clapped eyes of the couple, I wondered how long it would take for Grandma to say "See ya later, boy" to her new beau.

My best friend, Bree and my brother, Craig, were probably the only people other than Liam and myself that were even vaguely sober. They sat opposite us and were whispering sweet nothings in that sickening way normal people do when they are in love. Officially, I was happy for them, but even after a year or so, it still felt a little weird to see my best friend, who I felt was more like a sister to me than a friend, and my brother together in an intimate relationship. Seeing them kissing was a sort of pseudo-incestuous display, and we had more than enough of *that* during Christmas two years ago when that whole incident with Grandma Flo and my cousin happened. As a family, we collectively decided to NEVER bring that up again. The whole thing was just too disturbing to contemplate.

Despite the revolting cocktails and the frightening displays of naked uncle flesh, everything was going fairly smoothly. Everyone was having a good time, getting along with each other and there had been no trips to the emergency room. Perhaps the temporary rebranding of Christmas to our bachelor party / wedding had somehow cast out the evil spirits that usually inhabited this house during the holiday season. Or perhaps just thinking such thoughts was tempting fate, and the universe was simply biding it's time for an opportunity to inflict maximum destruction upon us all.

Now that's what I call the Christmas spirit.

"Yoo hoo, everyone!" my mother called out from the other end of the patio, "I have a little announcement. I wasn't sure if they were going to be able to make it, but we have a couple of surprise guests!"

With that, Mum stepped aside to reveal a man and a woman looking around the patio sporting equal expressions of horror and disgust.

My heart froze and I immediately looked at Liam. He had gone white as a sheet. My mother had done some stupid, ill-conceived and just downright deranged things in her time, but Kathleen Nolan had certainly outdone herself this time. She had crossed a line I thought even she wouldn't be insane enough to cross.

My mother had invited Liam's parents to our wedding.

Chapter Seven – The Fight

I WAS MOMENTARILY stunned by the unexpected appearance of Liam's parents. Of all the horrific and disastrous events that I could have imagined happening tonight, what was unraveling before my eyes right now had never, in my wildest dreams, crossed my mind.

Robert and Marilyn Brighton, Liam's parents, stood motionless at the other end of the patio, silently observing the scene before them. Dressed in exquisite designer outfits more befitting a night at the opera than a backyard bachelor party, the couple could not have looked more out of place if they had tried. The fact they had elected to attend despite having no relationship with Liam, myself or my family was a baffling choice on their part. Why my mother had thought it appropriate to invite these people considering Liam having made it clear, on multiple occasions, that he had gone 'no contact' with them years earlier left me equally confused.

Irregardless of her motivations, I was furious with my mother.

Robert's face was impassive, with only his narrowed eyes betraying his haughty sense of derision for the group of people before him. A group whom, I had no doubt, he would have no compunction labelling as 'classless trash' and beneath him in every conceivable way.

His wife was not so controlled. Marilyn's face was a picture of undisguised fury. Her features were scrunched up, as if assaulted by some unseen, acrid aroma; her delicately sculpted eyebrows furrowed in a deep scowl. Her eyes flashed as she scornfully stared at the man she once called her son.

"I knew you had become a degenerate, Liam," Marilyn hissed, looking her son up and down with disgust, "But I had no idea you had fallen this far to make such a public spectacle of yourself."

I snapped out of my state of shock and looked over at my sister, who was immediately regretting her choice of bachelor party prank, as Liam and I stood before them in our matching go-go dancer outfits.

"I beg your pardon?" I said, stepping forward, "Who the hell do you think you're calling a degenerate?"

"Stay out of this, you!" Robert barked, "This is between us and our son."

I opened my mouth to reply, but Liam placed his hand on my shoulder, stopping me in my tracks. He gently gestured me aside and he moved toward his parents.

"What are you doing here?" Liam asked, his voice low and gentle, and I knew from that tone that Liam was desperately trying to hold onto his temper.

"We're here to put an end to this nonsense once and for all," Marilyn said, "Before you embarrass us any more than you already have. I won't have you ruining our family's good name with your revolting debauchery and unwholesome associations." she said, casting a discourteous eye around the patio.

Liam rolled his eyes and chuckled mirthlessly.

"Listen you your mother, Liam." Robert boomed, clearly enraged that his son was not immediately coming to heel.

"No, you listen to me!" Liam roared and it was the first time I had heard him raise his voice – ever. His parents were clearly shocked too, as they took a step back, flinching at his tone.

"Who the hell do you think you are? Coming here making demands and throwing around insults? You're nothing to me. Nothing. Any chance of us having any kind of relationship ended when you turned your back on Rory in his hour of need. You couldn't even bring yourselves to attend your own son's funeral. And all because it might have made you look bad in the society pages." Liam was barely containing himself as he spat his words at them like acid. Marilyn looked like she had been slapped, while her husband turned bright red, though not from embarrassment. He was clearly not the kind of man who was accustomed to being given such a public dressing-down as he was currently receiving from his son.

"And you have the audacity to come here and call me *degenerate*? You have no place here and you sure as fuck have no place in my life anymore. Now unless you want me to contact the media with a juicy tell-all story about what growing up with the two of you as my parents was *really* like, I suggest you get the hell out of here and don't ever come back. As far as I'm concerned, you're both dead to me."

The patio was silent. Robert turned on his heel and stormed away, leaving his wife looking pale, her mouth agape as she tried to form words.

"Like he said," my father said coldly, stepping forward, "I think it's time you were leaving."

Marilyn looked around the patio at a sea of faces that were distinctly unfriendly and unsympathetic to her cause. She flushed with what I can only assume was shame at her abject failure to accomplish whatever it was she was hoping to achieve here tonight.

"This isn't over! You won't get away with this!" she snarled defiantly in a meagre attempt to save face, then turned and joined her husband in a hasty departure.

I let out a breath and put my hand on Liam's back to support him, as he took a few deep breaths and wiped a few stray tears from his face. Well, it seems we have a new contender for Worst Nolan Family Christmas ever – and we're only a few hours into the festivities. That's gotta be a record. I was about to share my thoughts in the hopes it might lighten the mood, but the words died on my tongue when I saw the expression on Liam's face. His features were cold and stony as he looked across the patio and zeroed in on my mother.

"Liam, maybe we should go upstairs and get changed?" I said gently, but he moved away and approached Kathleen Nolan with slow, deliberate steps. Liam had been angry when he had been speaking with his parents, but this was far worse. This was a sort of cold fury mixed with something else I couldn't quite place.

"Explain." Liam said, his voice barely above a whisper.

"I... I don't know what you mean..." Mum said.

"Explain!" Liam said, this time his tone a lot sharper.

"I don't know!" Mum said, sounding almost panicked, "I didn't think this was going to happen! I thought I was doing a good thing!"

"A good thing?"

"Yes! I just thought if your parents got the chance to see their son get married, it might help to heal the rift between you. I thought they would see what a lovely boy you are and everything would work itself out." Mum said, and even I could tell she was clutching at straws.

I suspected she hadn't fully thought her plans through before getting carried away with this whole wedding hoopla. Like previous Christmases, Mum's obsessive need for a 'perfect' celebration had somehow lead to this moment – and only when the Brightons had shown up had she fully realised what a catastrophic mistake she had made.

Liam stopped directly in front of my mother and looked down into her wide eyes. He stood motionless as he appeared to carefully consider his words. When he finally spoke, Liam's voice was soft and deliberate.

"Kathleen, do you remember the day shortly after Christmas last year? You and I met up at that restaurant in the city for lunch and we spent the afternoon catching up. Do you remember how we eventually ended up talking about my past?"

Mum nodded but said nothing.

"I told you how I felt about my parents. About the way they used to treat me and my brother when we were growing up. Like the two of us were just fashion accessories rather than children. And how, when we grew up, my parents only seemed to care about us not 'embarrassing' them by doing anything that their society friends might consider inappropriate or classless."

Mum was lost for words, but she continued to nod her agreement, but she appeared to be finding it difficult to continue to meet Liam's eyes.

"And after what they did to my brother... how they abandoned him when he needed them the most. How they pretended that he never existed..." Liam momentarily lost his composure as a sob escaped him, "I told you I *never* wanted anything to do with those people ever again. I told you they were no longer part of my life."

I put my arm around Liam's shaking shoulders, silently giving him support as my mother flushed bright red, a tear slipping down one cheek.

"I don't know why I'm even surprised. You doing this is just typical of your usual selfish, arrogant narcissism. All that matters... all that ever matters is what *you* want, Kathleen, and bugger everyone else's feelings. When it comes down to it, you're no better than my own mother."

"Now wait a minute..." Dad said, moving forward to defend his wife, but I shook my head at him, silently telling him to back off. He didn't like it, but he stepped back. Liam took a calming breath and continued.

"That day at the restaurant... that conversation we had... that was more of a mother/son relationship than I ever had with my own mother. So for you to invite those people here today, knowing my history with them? That was unforgivable. It was a fundamental betrayal and you can go straight to hell."

And with that, Liam turned away from Kathleen and headed inside the house. I followed close behind, passing my mother as she covered her face and wept.

Chapter Eight – The Aftermath

IN OUR ROOM upstairs, Liam and I quickly changed out of the ridiculous outfits my sister had duped us into wearing. Once back in our regular clothes, we lay down on the bed. I pressed myself up against Liam's back and wrapped myself protectively around him. A few moments later, I held him tighter as Liam began to weep silently, releasing all the pent-up emotion he'd kept buried for so long.

It wasn't just the incident downstairs with Mum that had triggered this. It wasn't even the confrontation with his parents earlier. Liam had never fully processed the trauma of his childhood; his parent's controlling and cruel nature, or the aftermath of his brother's death and Liam's rejection by his entire family. All that pain. All that loss. It had finally come back to the surface and Liam was now being forced to confront it head-on. I soothed my lover with gentle words and reassuring touches as he let years of grief and pain wash over him. When he finally calmed and his tears stopped, he patted my hand and assured me that he was okay.

"You don't have to be okay," I told him, giving him one last reassuring squeeze before letting him roll over to face me.

"Yeah, I know. I'm just not used to being so emotional."

"I'm not surprised. Your parents made it impossible for you to express yourself growing up. Say what you like about my family, but one thing we never do is repress our feelings." I said with a smirk.

"Oh god! Your mother!" Liam said, covering his face with his hands in what I could only assume was embarrassment, "I said the most horrible things to her!"

"And most of them she deserved to hear. I love my mother, but sometimes she just doesn't understand the concept of personal boundaries. I know her heart is always in the right place, but she really needs to start listening to that little voice inside her head that's saying

'Maybe this is a bad idea' – especially if she doesn't want crap like this to blow up in her face all the time."

"And what about my parents?" Liam said, his face suddenly sombre, "Why do you think they said the things they said? Why are they like that?"

I pulled him back into another warm embrace, gently stroking his head as I spoke.

"I dunno. Maybe they're a product of their upbringing. Maybe they behave the way they do because they've never had anyone stand up to them before. Or maybe, just maybe, they're a pair of mean-spirited old arseholes who you're better off without."

Liam laughed, and it felt good to cheer him up, even if I knew that it would take a long time for him to truly process everything. A little lighthearted banter was good for the soul.

"My blow-up with your Mum was still pretty brutal. Do you think she'll forgive me?"

"Oh, please! As Nolan family arguments go, it was pretty tame. Remind me to tell you the story about the fight between Mum and Aunt Joss at Easter a few years back. There's still a huge crack in the kitchen wall. Mum covers it up with that hideous calendar with the kitten pictures on it."

Liam looked at me like I, or perhaps my entire family were certifiably insane. Like the events of the last couple of years weren't evidence enough.

"Come on. Let's go downstairs and sort it out. One thing about this family, we stick together. No matter how many fights we have."

Liam and I headed downstairs to a melancholy scene. Most of the family were still out on the patio, but the crowd was unusually quiet, clearly rattled by everything that had happened earlier. We found Mum sitting at the kitchen table, her face tired and streaked from dried tears that had ruined her normally immaculately applied make-up. Dad was sitting by her side, holding her hand. Mum looked up as we entered the room, her eyes going wide.

"Can we talk for a second?" Liam asked hesitantly as he stepped forward. Mum nodded and stood up, clearly unsure as to what was about to happen. Liam simply opened his arms and that was all the invitation she needed. Mum stepped into his embrace and began crying again, repeatedly mumbling apologies against Liam's chest.

"I know, I know. I'm sorry too" Liam quietly repeated as he held my mother close, squeezing her reassuringly, as he silently shed a few more tears as well.

I knew how much Liam loved my mother. Despite her flaws, she had never been anything but open and loving toward him. I also knew the thought of losing her because of some stupid fight had rattled him way more than whatever shrill bullshit his parents had said earlier.

"How about I make us all some tea?" I suggested once Liam and my mother calmed themselves and sat down at the kitchen table, "It's been a long night and tomorrow is a big day."

And it would be. For tomorrow, I would be marrying the man of my dreams.

Chapter Nine – Wedding Balls

December 24th – Christmas Eve + The Big Day

THE NEXT MORNING, Mum was out on the patio when Liam and I came downstairs, busy setting everything up for the wedding ceremony. All the curtains and blinds were closed to obscure our view of the patio and backyard, Mum having explained the night before that we wouldn't be allowed to see anything until the ceremony. When Kathleen Nolan uttered the words 'it's a surprise' I felt a familiar cold chill run down my spine.

We made our way to the kitchen where my Dad was busy whipping up breakfast. I poured us some coffee and sat down at the table as Dad presented Liam and I with two plates of... something.

"Um, what is it?" I asked as I experimentally poked the wobbling pile of goo with a fork.

"Omelettes," Dad replied like it was an utterly ridiculous question.

"I thought the Australian Egg Marketing Board got a court injunction preventing you from making omelettes again?" I snarked.

"You're far too critical. My omelettes aren't that bad?"

"Why are they bright green?" Liam asked.

"It's the spinach. I think I added too much. Besides, you're both being very insulting to my excellent kitchen skills!"

"I'm sorry, Dad," I said with as much mock seriousness as I could muster, "Congratulations on yet another culinary masterpiece. Way to subvert society's expectations of what an omelette should look like. Two thumbs up!"

"It's too early in the morning for your shitting sarcasm," Dad grumbled as he began whipping up more green grossness, clearly determined to create a perfect emerald eggstravaganza.

"It's never too early for my shitting sarcasm," I smirked as I tasted a mouthful of the obscene omelette. It looked awful, but taste-wise, it was actually quite disgusting.

"You're not too old to put over my knee, young man!" Dad snapped.

"Sorry, Dad. That's Liam's job now." I said as Liam blushed.

"Charlie! A father doesn't need to imagine his son like that!"

"Well, that's what you get for serving me green eggs and ham on my wedding day.

Thankfully our revolting repast was interrupted when Mum appeared in the kitchen looking as flustered as she usually did on Christmas Eve, but with a bonus stress-induced eye twitch added to the mix.

"Alright, you two. Upstairs with you!" she said with a clap.

"What's happening now?" Liam asked, looking faintly relieved he wouldn't have to eat the rest of his omelette.

"I've laid out your outfits for the ceremony upstairs, along with everything you'll need for the big day!"

"Crucifix, holy water, wooden stake..." I muttered under my breath. Mum narrowed her eyes but ignored me.

"Come on, love." Liam whispered in my ear, "Let's go get ready. The sooner we get married, the sooner we can get to the wedding night!" he said salaciously. I blushed at the thought and practically dragged my man upstairs. It was time to get this show on the road.

~

"Is she out of her fucking mind?!?" I cried as I stepped into the bedroom. My thoughts of sexy, kinky wedding nights instantly evaporated when Liam and I were confronted by what was quite possibly the most hideous sights imaginable.

Laid out on the bed were two transparent plastic garment bags containing our 'outfits' for the wedding. Both contained trousers, shirts, waistcoats and jackets. Both had either been picked out by someone with a serious vision disorder, or possibly the ghost of Dame Barbara Cartland.

I've got to hand it to my mother. When she said she was going to plan a gay wedding, it wasn't an idle threat. Based on these outfits alone, there was absolutely no possibility that anyone would mistake us for anything other than a gay couple in these disturbing matching outfits.

Each ensemble consisted of Barbie pink trousers and long-tailed jackets, tastelessly combined with gold sequin lame waistcoats that looked like something stolen from a Studio 54 disco diva's talent manager. The whole thing was accented with plum pocket squares and neon pink cravats. Liam and I looked at each other with horror.

"Did you know about this?" I accused.

"I knew she organised outfits, but not this! My god, it actually hurts my eyes!" he squinted, "This has got to be your sister pulling another prank."

"My sister is capable of a great many things, but I can't imagine a reality where she would willingly go into a shop and buy anything pink. She's not exactly a girly girl. Besides, this absolute abomination has Mum written all over it."

Ever since we announced our engagement, Mum had made a huge deal about us having a 'gay' wedding. I guess this was what she meant. It didn't matter how many times we had made it clear that, as a couple, we preferred to focus on the 'wedding' bit rather than the 'gay' bit; that it was enough for there to be two grooms and no brides; Mum seemed to feel that our big day needed to make a statement. And apparently, that statement was 'Yaaaas, Kween!'

Honestly, though. Would it have killed her to just pick out a couple of normal tuxedos? Why did she have to dress us up in clothes that would make Liam and I look like a pair of flaming flamingo haemorrhoids?

In a last-ditch effort to try and tone down our outfits, we raided our luggage in the hopes of finding something to soften Mum's vision slightly. Unfortunately, since neither of us had packed with the idea of emergency last-minute matrimonial attire modification in mind, we were pretty much screwed. Although, at this stage, we could probably put on the bachelor party costumes my sister provided and manage to look less eye-catching.

"Thirty-minute curtain call, boys!" Mum called out from downstairs. "Hurry up! You don't want to be late for your own wedding!"

I shuddered at the thought of actually being seen in such visually offensive garments, but with no other options available and time working against us, Liam and I began stripping off our clothes and changing into our pink power suits. When I was done, I turned to the mirror and gazed at myself in horror.

I looked like a giant piece of bubblegum that had coughed up a strawberry milkshake.

"It's not that bad," Liam said with absolutely no conviction.

"Really?"

"It could be worse."

"Are you out of your mind? You can't say things like that. You'll jinx us!" I hissed. Liam just smirked at me.

"If we can look at each other in these outfits and still want to go through with the wedding, or without going blind, I think we'll be just fine. You do still want to go through with it, right?"

"You better believe it, my love. Even if I'm dressed like Lady Gaga's tax accountant."

Liam chuckled and gave me a swift kiss. "Then let's get down there before your mother starts without us!"

So Liam and I joined hands and made our way downstairs toward the biggest event of our lives. When we got to the back of the house, we saw the curtains covering the entrance to the patio had been opened, which I took as a sign we were free to come outside. When we stepped onto the patio, it was like time stopped. What greeted us was unlike anything either one of us could have imagined in a million years of fever dreams.

"Holy crap!" Liam breathed, "Is she for real?"

My mother had promised us a gay wedding. She had delivered.

Chapter Ten – The Gayest Wedding in the Universe

IT TOOK A few seconds for my eyes to adjust. It was a bit like being at the flashpoint of a nuclear explosion, except brighter and with more glitter. The patio had been converted into a reception hall. The long dining table had been shifted to one end, allowing room at the other for a deejay booth and dance floor.

The garden had been set up for the ceremony itself, with an altar and rows of chairs where our family and friends were seated. Uncle Jack was dressed as a giant red love heart, with a rainbow sash tied around his midsection. He was holding what looked like a very expensive digital camera and was busy snapping pictures of the altar, the wedding guests and us when our eyes met.

Bree was standing with my brother at the back of the seating area, dressed in a voluminous and frilly pink dress that made her look vaguely like Little Bo Peep, but since I quite preferred my testicles attached to my body, I decided it would be best if I never shared that passing thought with her. Bree was holding a large woven basket, overflowing with rose petals, which told me the battle over who would be the flower girl had been fought and won. I wondered if Uncle Jack would ever recover from such a devastating defeat.

All of this would be fine – except for the genuinely disturbing amount of glitter, sequins, disco balls and rainbow pride flags that now adorned every conceivable surface. The wooden posts that surrounded the patio, along with the roof beams above us, had been wrapped in a combination of pink feather boas and rainbow twinkle lights. It gave the effect of a Muppet pole dancing while having a seizure.

The dining table had been set with a gaudy silver lame tablecloth, polished chrome candelabras and what appeared to be metal dildos that were being used as place card holders. At the other end of the patio, a truly ludicrous lighting rig had been installed above the dance floor – something that was designed for a nightclub rather than a small backyard – along with dozens of shimmering mirror balls of various sizes.

My parents were standing in the middle of the garden, circulating amongst the guests near the altar. On one side were four muscular men wearing skimpy black leather shorts and harnesses across their oiled chests. On the other, four drag queens who were wearing what was easily the most hideous, eye-wateringly awful full-length rainbow ball gowns in the history of fashion; a visual cacophony that seemed to make even them wince. I didn't recognise any of these people and briefly wondered what these strangers were doing at my wedding.

So to summarise, if I were asked to describe the overall aesthetic of my wedding, it would be something akin to a gay cruise ship crashing into a gay pride parade on the planet Homosexual. It was clear the word *subtle* was not in my mother's vocabulary.

For the first time in my life, I was speechless.

"Welcome to your wedding, boys! What do you think?" Mum called out triumphantly, clearly proud of designing a gay wedding so gay, it would make Mr Humphries from *Are You Being Served?* Say 'Bitch, please – nobody's this bloody queer!' I tried to say something, but it was like something in my brain had short-circuited and I just couldn't form words. Liam didn't look much better, but I could tell he was desperately trying to come up with something positive to say and was failing miserably.

"This is…" I started, trying desperately to not sound ungrateful, "Words fail me!"

Mum looked delighted. "I knew you'd love it!" she crowed, dragging my father off to fuss over the decorations on the altar.

"Um, well…" I tried to say, but it was far too late. Mum was off in her own little world, leaving Liam and I baffled and unsure how to proceed.

The last thing I wanted to do was hurt my Mum's feelings and, honestly, as much as I wanted to be grateful for the enormous effort she had put in, this was just about the most offensive wedding I could possibly imagine.

Don't get me wrong. I'm all for celebrating my sexuality. I'm a proud gay man and have never denied my true self. I was blessed to have been born into a family that loved and accepted me for who I am without a moment's hesitation. While I have always appreciated my parent's unconditional love, there are times when my mother's almost psychotic attempts to celebrate *'my culture'* crossed the line when it came to taste, decency or sanity.

Today was definitely one of those times.

It was then I noticed that one of the drag queens by the altar was, on closer inspection, vaguely familiar to me. It took me a moment to place her face, but I finally remembered her from a nightclub I'd gone to a few years ago. Her name was Fanny La Queef. Although, that didn't explain what she was doing in my parent's backyard on my wedding day.

"Excuse me? Hi!" I said as I approached the statuesque queen, who was wearing an enormous blonde beehive wig covered in rainbow butterfly clips. I wondered briefly if butterflies hung around beehives, or if this was the drag queen equivalent of a mixed metaphor. I thought it best not to ask.

"Hi, Sugar!" Fanny La Queef said in a deep, baritone voice that was somewhat incongruous to her otherwise ultra-feminine countenance.

"I know this is going to sound like a stupid question, but what are you doing here?" I asked. Fanny let out a throaty chuckle as if I had, in fact, asked the stupidest questions imaginable.

"I'm your Maid of Honour!"

"And we're your bridesmaids!" the other drag queens cooed in unison.

Because of course, they were. Which meant the leather boys across the aisle were... I met Liam's gaze and his eyes went wide when the penny finally dropped.

That was it. Time out.

"Mum!" I shouted, probably a little louder than I had intended, if the startled looks on everyone's faces were anything to go by. Mum came dashing over, looking a little panicked, Dad bringing up the rear.

"Don't you just love it all, Charlie? I think everything came together quite nicely!" she said in a voice that sounded more than a little manic.

"Are you kidding, Mum?" I said, desperately trying to remain calm and avoid yet another traditional Nolan Family disaster. "No, I can't say I do love it. What the hell were you thinking?"

"You don't like it?" Mum asked, sounding unsure for the first time.

"Um, let's take a look at our outfits or, better yet, the bridesmaid's outfits. Oh, by the way – why the fuck have I got bridesmaids? I'm not a bride!"

"Charlie, maybe you should take a breath?" Liam suggested, desperately trying to calm me, but I was having none of it.

"Why? Why all of this? Why couldn't we have a nice, simple, elegant ceremony? Why did you have to turn our wedding day into this ridiculous big gay joke!"

"It's your culture, Charlie!" Mum defended, but she had played right into my hands. I may not be the bride, but my mother was about to get a full-blown faceful of Bridezilla fury.

"Since when is my culture a drag queen Maid of Honour called Fanny La Queef? Since when is my culture a tacky explosion of rainbow pride flags and feather boas? Since when is my culture leather boys in bondage gear? Who the hell are these people, anyway? Why are they in our bridal party?"

"I hired them! I didn't really have much of a choice, since none of your friends would agree to wear the outfits!"

How my mother didn't interpret this as a giant blaring warning siren that her plans may require some serious retooling, I'll never understand. But then again, Kathleen Nolan's internal alarm bells stopped working a very long time ago.

"Now, Son, your mother has put a lot of effort into planning the perfect gay wedding for you," Dad said.

"And that's the problem right there, Dad. Mum's so fixated on it being a *gay* wedding, rather than just making it a wedding. I mean, for crying out loud! Have you ever seen me wear anything like this before? So why the hell would I want to look like some glittering gay peacock on my wedding day?" I was nearly hysterical, and I tried to catch my breath, but I was well on my way to a full-blown panic attack.

I knew it was too much to expect just one Nolan Family event to avoid falling into a spiral of lunacy and screaming matches. The family that could turn a game of hopscotch into a bloodbath was never going to be able to pull off a wedding without it descending into a catastrophe.

"Well, I think you're being very ungrateful, young man!" Mum said with as much vitriol as I had ever heard from her.

And I saw red.

"UNGRATEFUL?" I hissed venomously, momentarily losing the ability to string together the words needed to express just how outraged I was at that moment.

"Now just a minute, Kathleen!" Grandma Flo interjected, walking up the aisle with determination – and I was utterly flabbergasted at her appearance. My grandmother, whose normal idea of a fancy outfit was adding a brooch to her ever-present oversized cardigan or muumuu, was dressed in a gold sequined minidress and white thigh-high go-go boots. She wore a sparkling gold glitter-coated bishop's hat and a black leather choker around her neck. It was then I realised that this was my mother's coup de grace.

Grandma Flo was officiating the wedding ceremony.

She took a moment to salaciously ogle the semi-naked leather boys that stood behind us, then turned her attention to her daughter.

"I told you to clear all this with the boys before locking anything in. You can't blame them for being shocked when you go ahead and spring all this on them without any warning!"

"How was I supposed to clear it with them, Mother? It was supposed to be a surprise!"

"Why? Who had a surprise wedding, Kathleen? What's next, a surprise funeral?" Grandma Flo said with exasperation.

"Keep it up, old woman, I'll give you a surprise funeral!" Mum seethed.

"Don't talk to Grandma like that!" Charmaine yelled, standing up from her seat in the audience and barreling forward to defend our grandmother.

"You stay out of this, young lady!" Dad reprimanded.

"She can do whatever she wants. I'm the bride and I command it!" I yelled.

Wait. Did I really just call myself the bride? Fuck me, dead...

"I agree," Liam chimed in calmly, "and Kathleen, Charlie's right. This is all far, far too much. We appreciate the effort you've gone o, but this isn't a wedding. It's an offensive stereotype explosion. If we're going to do this, I think we need to tone everything down. I don't want *this* to be what we look back on as our special day."

Mum visibly deflated at Liam's words.

"Is it really that bad?" Mum said, her voice barely above a whisper.

"It's the thought that counts," I said, moving forward and pulling my mother into a big hug to reassure her. "But you've got to admit, this is all completely ridiculous."

"Truer words were never spoken." A woman's voice called out from the far end of the garden. We turned to see Liam's parents along with two police officers approaching the altar.

"I have a court order to stop this wedding immediately!" Robert boomed, waving a stack of papers around that he held in his hand.

"Officers, arrest that man!" Marilyn shrieked, pointing her immaculately manicured finger directly at me.

"Okay, everyone," I said, looking around the garden with resignation. "Which one of you said *'Well, at least this day couldn't get any worse'*? Be honest."

Chapter Eleven – My In-Laws Make My Family Seem Quite Normal

THE POLICE OFFICERS approached me, their expressions stern, and told me I was under arrest. I stood there bewildered as they told me to turn around and place my hands behind my back.

"Mum? Dad? What the hell are you doing back here?" Liam shouted.

"Why are you arresting my son?" Mum cried, barreling forward in a futile attempt to shield me from the law enforcement officers. "What's he being charged with?"

A part of me briefly thought about the hideous outfit I was wearing and wondered if I was being charged with crimes against fashion. It would be hard to deny such an accusation.

"Child abduction and human trafficking." one officer, who was apparently the senior of the two, said solemnly.

"What the hell are you talking about?" I squawked, panic overtaking me as my arms were secured behind my back with a snap of the handcuffs.

This was totally insane.

"Mrs Brighton has filed a report claiming you abducted her child and are in the process of forcing the child into an illegal child marriage. The law takes a dim view of such matters." The second officer said as he patted me down, presumably in case I was hiding any bazookas or illegal fireworks on my person.

"The law must be pretty dim in general if you swallowed that load of old codswallop!" Mum said acidly.

"Um, newsflash! This is her child!" I waved my handcuffed hands as best I could in Liam's direction. Liam was scowling at his parents with such unrelenting fury, that I was genuinely astonished they hadn't been reduced to dust and blown away on the summer breeze.

The two police officers froze.

"I beg your pardon, sir?" The senior officer asked, suddenly realising this situation was not as straightforward as he had been led to believe.

"And don't you usually have to conduct some kind of investigation BEFORE you go ahead and arrest someone? What the hell is wrong with you?" Liam scolded, "Uncuff him this instant if you don't want to get sued into the middle of next century!"

"Hang on a minute!" the senior officer said, turning to me. "My sergeant told us to head over here and bring you in based on the sworn statement made by Mrs Brighton."

"Well, I guess that makes Mrs Brighton a lying old bitch who's about to get thrown in jail, now doesn't it!" Grandma Flo said, giving Marilyn a one-fingered salute and blowing a raspberry. Proof, if ever it were needed, that age and maturity did not walk hand in hand.

"Officers!" Marilyn cried, clearly not happy with how this preposterous plan of hers was imploding before her eyes. "Stop dilly-dallying and get on with it. Don't listen to these... people." She said that last word with all the disdain she could muster. "I don't have all day. I'm a busy woman!"

"I'd clear your schedule if I were you, Mother," Liam said. "The pair of you have finally gone too far. What you've done here is blatantly illegal, and I'm done with you interfering with my life. We've had nothing to say to each other since Rory died and, as far as I'm concerned, you are no longer my parents."

"We still have a court order!" Robert called out, waving documents around as if they were some kind of trump card. "This wedding is over. We won't have you humiliating us in front of the whole of Melbourne with your disgusting, deviant nonsense."

"Your so-called court order is entirely fraudulent. Even if you managed to get one of your Judge friends to sign off on this absolute idiocy, it's based on knowingly false information. How did you think you were going to get away with this?" I said.

"Oh, please!" Robert said, sounding equally snide and arrogant. "The law isn't for people like you. It's for your betters. I have a high-priced legal team that will put an end to this matter before it ever makes it to court."

It was then I noticed Grandma Flo and Uncle Jack whispering furiously amongst themselves. Jack gestured to his camera before the two of them quickly dashed off into the house. Meanwhile, Liam snatched the bundle of papers out of his father's hand and quickly tore then up.

"I don't think so, sir." The senior police officer said as I heard the click of my handcuffs as they were removed, finally releasing my aching wrists. "I think you and your wife can accompany us down to the station for a little chat. I have a feeling my sergeant is going to have a lot of questions for you too."

The shocked expression on the faces of Liam's parents almost made this whole fiasco worth it, as the two police officers approached them and began to escort them away.

"You can't do this to us! Don't you know who I am?" Marilyn cried with indignation.

"I'll end your careers for this!" Robert screamed at the officers as he was forcibly dragged away after refusing to move voluntarily, his face bright red with fury. "I have a team of lawyers!"

"You're going to need them," Liam said sadly, deflating as he watched his parents escorted away and bundled into the waiting police car outside.

"Are you okay?" I asked as I wrapped him up in a big hug.

"Yeah, I suppose. If I ever needed proof my relationship with my parents was dead and buried, I think I got it today. At least I have some closure now. But what about you? Are you okay? How are your wrists?"

"Oh, I'm fine," I said, rubbing my wrists. "It's funny, I always had a fantasy about getting cuffed by a cop. The reality, however, didn't live up to the hype."

Liam chuckled. "Don't worry. When we get finished with today, we'll explore some much more fun fantasies," he said, waggling his eyebrows salaciously.

Grandma Flo and Uncle Jack appeared looking almost manic with their matching smiles. I had a feeling these two had been up to no good, and I was here for it.

"What have you two been up to?" I said.

"Well, my darling Charlie," Grandma said, looking mischievous as always. "Let's just call it an early wedding gift. Show them, Jack!"

Uncle Jack smirked and turned his digital camera around to show us the small display on the back. On it was an image of Liam's parents being dragged toward a police car; their faces twisted in abject fury.

"Oh my god!" I gasped as Liam grinned and grabbed the camera to take a close look at the image.

"I had a feeling something huge was about to go down." Grandma Flo explained, "So I dragged Jack out the front with his camera in the hopes of snapping a Kodak moment. And boy did we get one!" she cackled wildly.

"Can you send this to me please, Jack?" Liam asked, his eyes not leaving the tiny display.

"Sure thing, kid." Uncle Jack chuckled.

"I have a feeling this picture might just get anonymously sent to a few friends of mine in the local news media. My parents always loved it when they made the society pages. So I can only imagine they'll be absolutely delighted with a full-page spread and write-up."

I smiled evilly at Liam as he gave me a wide-eyed look of innocence. My man could be a real bitch sometimes. And I couldn't be more in love with him if I tried.

"So, shall we get married?" I asked.

"We shall. But I've had a thought." Liam turned to the assembled guests who were now crowded around the garden. "Everyone! Grab a chair and prepare to follow me."

"Where are we going?"

"Well, first, you and I are getting changed. Then, we're going to do this right," he said, giving me a quick kiss and taking my hand as he ushered me upstairs.

Chapter Twelve – Putting the Hitch in Getting Hitched

WHEN WE GOT upstairs, Liam sent a few quick text messages before raiding our suitcases. While I couldn't be happier to be stripping out of the gaudy pink abominations my mother had provided us with, I did wonder what my fiance had planned as replacement outfits.

"I'm sure your Dad won't mind if we borrow these," Liam said as he grabbed a couple of white button-up shirts from my parent's wardrobe. He handed me one along with a pair of black beach shorts he'd plucked from my bag.

"Any chance you're gonna fill me in on your plans?" I asked with amusement as I started undressing.

"Wasn't this supposed to be a surprise wedding?" he replied cheekily. The look of horror on my face must have been obvious as he quickly moved to reassure me. "Don't worry. This will be a surprise you're going to love, I promise."

Once we were both dressed, I looked at myself in the full-length mirror. While I never imagined getting married in board shorts and a baggy shirt, I couldn't help but feel the mixture of casual and formal was somehow fitting and reflective of us as a couple.

A noise from outside caught my attention and I glanced out the bedroom window, down at the front yard. My family we're migrating en masse across the lawn, carrying everything from chairs to bits of the altar, moving everything down the street on foot. It was then I realised Liam's plan.

My man was a genius.

~

Such a simple and elegant solution. My family and friends were gathered together in what was probably the most perfect wedding venue I could ever have hoped for. I closed my eyes and embraced the scent of salt in the air; the light sea breeze keeping us cool despite the heat of the Summer sun beaming down on us; and the feeling of sand beneath my bare feet. It was glorious.

A simple wedding ceremony down on the quiet little beach a few minutes walk from my parent's house – why hadn't I thought of that earlier? While Liam and I had been changing our outfits, our guests had quickly relocated down to the cove, setting up the chairs and wedding altar in a nice spot overlooking the shimmering blue ocean. No disco balls. No drag queens. No metal dildos. Just the people we love and the beauty of nature.

I stood in front of our guests opposite the man I love, grinning uncontrollably as Grandma Flo stepped forward to perform the ceremony. She too had changed her outfit, losing the gold mini dress and go-go boots but, curiously, she had retained the giant gold bishop's hat.

"Um, Grandma? Why are you still wearing that?" I asked hesitantly.

"It took me three days to make this bloody thing. I got glitter in my eyes and burned myself on the hot glue gun. I'm wearing it!" she huffed.

I decided not to argue with her. If she wanted to wear a funny hat at my wedding, I could live with it.

"Dearly Beloved! We are gathered here today on this beach to join together Charlie and Liam in the bonds of marriage..." Grandma began. I must admit, I kind of tuned out a bit, as I was distracted by the look of absolute joy on the face of my darling Liam. His eyes were shining as he gazed upon me like I was the most amazing thing in the world. Probably mirroring my expression as I stared at this handsome man I was so lucky to love.

"If anyone has any reason that these two men should not be joined together, speak now or forever hold their peace."

"I object!" Charmaine called out, as everyone gasped in unison.

I slowly turned to my soon-to-be-dead sister and gave her a withering stare that had the potential to melt the putrid flesh from her bones.

"Only joking!" she said with a nervous giggle. "What? It wouldn't be a Nolan Family event without a little drama!"

I turned to my sister's girlfriend with a wicked smile on my face and the way Charmaine's expression fell, she realised she had fucked up royally.

"So, Robyn," I said cheerfully. "That trip my sister took to the Gold Coast after high school…"

"I'm sorry!" Charmaine barked out in a panic. "I'll be good, I swear!"

The guests laughed as Charmaine quietly sunk into her seat, Robyn pinching her on the arm for being a menace to society. I decided now was not the time for revenge. That would come later. I returned my attention to Liam and nodded to Grandma Flo to continue.

"Liam, do you take Charlie to be your husband, to have and to hold, in good times and in bad, as long as you both shall live?"

"I do," Liam said, and it was then I realised we had overlooked something crucial.

"Oh my god! We haven't got wedding rings! I didn't even think about that before now." I whispered, but Liam smiled a knowing smile.

"Well, actually, your Mum picked this out for you to give to Liam." Grandma Flo said, handing me an elegant white gold wedding band. It was simple but beautiful. Of all the choices Mum had made while organising the wedding, this was the only one I couldn't fault her on. I carefully slipped it onto Liam's finger and marvelled at how it sparkled in the Summer sun.

"And for you, Charlie…" Grandma said, waving her hand toward Liam, who pulled out a small black velvet ring box from his pocket, smiling broadly. He opened the box and I gasped as I immediately recognised the gorgeous antique wedding band. Similar to the one Grandma had just handed to me, this ring was also white gold, but with a tiny Argyle yellow diamond inset that looked like a drop of pure sunshine.

"I know for a fact your Grandpa would have been proud to see you wearing his ring, Charlie," Grandma whispered as I felt my eyes sting with unshed tears.

"Charlie, do you take Liam to be your husband, to have and to hold, in good times and in bad, as long as you both shall live?"

"I do!" I breathed excitedly. Liam slipped the wedding band onto my finger as we both grinned at each other with happy tears in our eyes.

"Then by the power vested in me by eWeddingChapel.com and the State of Victoria, I now pronounce you married. Charlie and Liam, you may now kiss each other!"

We didn't waste any more time, as we both leaned forward and allowed our lips to meet. Liam's hands moved up to frame my face as I ran my fingers through his hair. Our guests cheered and applause rang out across the beach, but all I focused on was the sweet taste of my husband.

My husband. Wow, that just has a nice ring to it.

~

After the ceremony, Uncle Jack took us aside to snap some photos. Some of just Liam and I, others with my parents and Grandma Flo. After our impromptu photo shoot, we all relocated back to my parent's house. While we had been away, Fanny La Queef, her fellow drag queens along with the leather boys had kindly agreed to do some minor redecorating of the patio area. While they couldn't perform any miracles in the time allotted, they did manage to tone down the more extreme elements of my mother's diabolical decorations. Gone were the metal dildos and the pride flags. The crop of disco balls had been drastically pruned back and the feather boas had been thinned out a little here and there. While not a drastic change by any means, it did manage to make things look a little less like the inside of Elton John's garden shed which, as far as I was concerned, was a win in my book.

Once everyone was settled, Liam and I took our place at the head of the table and grinned goofily at each other as we languished in our post-wedding ceremony joy, which was probably so saccharine sweet that every guest would develop a toothache before the end of the reception.

"Ladies and Gentlemen!" my mother called out from the back door. "In honour of this very special occasion, my husband and I would like to invite you all to join us in a drink to toast the happy couple!"

"Oh, fuck me dead!" I gasped in horror. "Mum, No! No more cocktails. I don't want my wedding day to feature any trips to the emergency room. Or the morgue!"

Mum looked at me like I was completely out of my mind, as she stepped aside to make way for my father who was carrying a magnum of champagne. I briefly felt embarrassed, but then I remembered that godawful cocktail my parents had served the year Liam and I reunited and felt no guilt at prejudging my mother in any way whatsoever.

The champagne bottle was opened with a thunderous firing of the cork, and my parents busied themselves filling glasses and handing them out to our guests. When she came over with two crystal flutes for Liam and me, she winked at me with a cheeky grin, silently letting me know that all was good between us and that despite the hiccups we had experienced today, my mother was very happy with how everything had turned out in the end. Although it was corny, I couldn't help but love it when Liam and I linked our arms and sipped the sparkling bubbly from each other's glasses.

After dinner was served, my brother took his place in the DJ booth and began playing a wonderful mix of modern dance tracks and classic retro tunes. Years ago, Craig had once worked as a mobile DJ performing at weddings and other private functions. He'd loved it but had ultimately given it up to serve his country in the armed forces. Now he was retired from the army, I wondered if he would go back to his old business. By the look on his face, he was having a whale of a time as he pressed buttons, swapped discs and bopped away in the booth as the beats rang out across the patio. My dear friend, Bree, stood alongside him, grinning like a fool as she watched her boyfriend do his thing.

"Ladies and Gentlemen!" Craig announced over the speakers, "Please clear the dance floor and make way for the happy couple, as they take their first dance!"

Oh, sweet baby cheeses. I hadn't thought of that. But Liam didn't seem to be phased in the slightest as he smiled, took my hand and gently guided me down to the other side of the patio. As we stood in the centre of the dance floor, a spotlight from the over-the-top lighting rig above us illuminated us like a searchlight.

"I don't think we need that, Craig!" I called out as I shielded my eyes with my hands. The light went out and my retinas slowly recovered from the nuclear flash. It was while I was regaining my eyesight that the music began and I froze on the spot. From out of the blur came a vision in rainbow and Miss Fanny La Queef took to the floor with a microphone in hand as she began to sing.

"Every night in my dreams, I see you, I feel you!" she boomed in her deep, baritone voice that made the drag queen sound a lot less like Celine Dion and closer to Barry White. Liam and I silently chuckled as our bodies began to sway. While personally, I would never have chosen *My Heart Will Go On for* the first dance at our wedding, at this point I would have been happy with *The Chicken Dance.*

So long as I was dancing with my Liam.

~

After we cut the wedding cake (an enormous, rainbow-coloured monstrosity Mum had ordered that could only have been made brighter with a bucket of kerosene and a match) and everyone was starting to relax into an alcohol and sugar-induced coma, Mum gathered all the single ladies and suggested it was time for me to *throw the bride's bouquet.*

This led to a slightly awkward back and forth where I was forced to reiterate to Mum, yet again, that not only was I not a bride, but that I hadn't had a bouquet at any point during the day. That's when Mum produced a small bouquet, thrust it upon me none too gently and hissed "Aim for your sister" in a way that sounded very much like it was a threat rather than a request. The fact Charmaine wasn't even remotely interested in marriage didn't seem to concern my mother in the slightest and arguing this point seemed like an exercise in futility. But since I still needed to get my sister back for that whole bachelor party/costume prank thing, not to mention that objection nonsense at the ceremony, I did what any good son would do.

I threw the bouquet as hard as I could and beaned my sister right in the face.

Charmaine scowled at my mother's squeal of delight that her daughter was going to be *'next'*. That scowl only deepened when my sister turned her incredulous expression toward me and saw what must have been quite the shit-eating grin.

"Well, on that note," I said, grabbing hold of Liam and unsubtly guiding him toward the house, "I think I need to drag the old ball-and-chain upstairs and make an honest man of him!"

"Ball-and-chain?" Liam repeated with disbelief.

"Oh, I can spend the weekend being called a *bride and* even a *slut in training*, but I call you a ball-and-chain and suddenly I'm crossing the line?"

"No, I just thought you were suggesting something kinky for our wedding night." Liam chuckled with a lecherous smirk that made my brain short-circuit.

"I'm sweet and innocent and I'm certain I have no idea what you're suggesting, dear husband!" I said with mock innocence, "But let's go before these lunatics drag us into more shenanigans."

And with that, we quietly slipped away.

~

Mum had quietly mentioned earlier that evening that my old room had been set up as a 'bridal suite' since spending our wedding night in my parent's bedroom was a little weird even for our family. When Liam and I got upstairs, we found my bedroom had been completely redecorated. The old bed had been replaced with a new queen-sized bed and made up with crisp white linen, lace and sprinkled generously with red rose petals. Vases of white lilies had been placed on every available surface and a bottle of chilled champagne was resting in an ice bucket on the bedside table along with two crystal flutes.

"Wow..." Liam breathed as he looked around the room.

"I know. Not a rainbow in sight." I said, making Liam laugh.

"Fancy a glass of bubbly?" Liam gestured to the ice bucket and I nodded enthusiastically. With a practised hand, my husband squeezed the cork out effortlessly and poured the sparkling liquid into the two waiting glasses.

"Are you trying to get me drunk?" I asked as we clinked glasses and took a sip.

"Nah, that's your parent's job. Besides, I'm pretty sure you're a safe bet."

"Pretty confident, aren't you?" I smirked.

"I sure am. I'm about to jump into bed with a married man."

"How outrageous of you!" I said as I emptied my glass, placed it down gently and took Liam in my arms. "Think you've got what it takes to seal the deal, huh?"

"Oh yes. I know exactly how to turn him on." Liam chuckled.

"Really? Tell me more."

"Well, today is Christmas Eve. So, from next year, it will also be our wedding anniversary too. That means from now on, we have a free pass to skip the usual Nolan Family Christmas insanity and we can celebrate on our own."

I moaned dramatically. "Oh my God! You know just what turns my crank! Take me now!" as we both laughed and threw ourselves onto the bed.

Epilogue – Christmas Day

WE WERE SO close. We almost achieved the impossible – a Nolan Family Christmas that didn't involve any fighting, screaming, explosive accusations or trips to the local emergency room. Everyone had been too happy enjoying Liam and I's wedding for the usual nonsense to come bubbling to the surface. Despite all the drama that had led up to the ceremony, the Nolan clan had collectively elected to leave their crazy pills at home and, against all odds, we were heading towards our most peaceful Christmas Day ever.

And then she did it. The mad woman tempted fate. In a moment of complete insanity, Mum suddenly remembered that we had forgotten something. An annual tradition that, because of our wedding distracting everyone, we had completely overlooked.

"We forgot about Games Night!" Mum cried out in the same tone of voice usually reserved for house fires and imminent death.

The whole family groaned their displeasure in unison.

Undeterred by our complete lack of enthusiasm, my mother – the sucker for punishment that she was – dashed out of the room with a slight skip in her step. Returning shortly afterwards baring the velvet bag that I now recognised as the harbinger of doom that it clearly was, Mum grinned manically as she plunged her hand into its murky interior. Evidently, it was time to select this year's method of Christmas disaster.

"Please, God, let it be Russian Roulette," I muttered under my breath.

"What?" Liam asked.

"Nothing," I said, realising I had let that one slip out loud.

Perhaps I was overreacting. Maybe it would be different this year. Sure, previous years had seen our family take innocent family party games such as *Twister, Eye Spy and Blind Man's Buff* and turn them into war crimes outlawed by the Geneva Convention. But this year was a rare exception, surely. Our wedding had used up all the craziness points and it would all be smooth sailing from here. Nothing could possibly disrupt our peaceful celebration of the birth of our Lord and Saviour.

"Trivial Pursuit!" Mum called out triumphantly as she read the folded piece of paper she had just plucked out of the velvet bag.

Shit.

"Absolutely Not!" I cried out, standing up and crossing my arms across my chest. "We are not going through that fucking nightmare again. Not after last time. Uncle Jack is still in therapy."

I pointed to Uncle Jack, who was sitting in the corner dressed as a Christmas star, rocking back and forth and mumbling to himself incoherently.

"Don't swear, Charlie! It's Christmas. It upsets the Baby Jesus." Mum said, scandalised.

"Again, I have to point out – we're not religious. So the Baby Jesus doesn't get a vote." I said, smirking.

"You know the rules, Charlie," Dad interjected, sounding resigned, "We have to play whatever your mother pulls out of the bag."

"Since when is swearing an issue, Mum?" Charmaine said. "We're hardly the bloody Brady Bunch, are we?"

"It's Christmas!" Mum said again as if this was explanation enough.

Oh dear. I could sense the tone shift around the room. It seemed this year, our annual game night was about to blow up even before the games had begun. This wasn't good.

"Yeah, sure," Aunt Joss slurred, having clearly been packing away more than her fair share of the cask wine since lunchtime. "Like we're the classiest family in the universe!"

"Well, we might be everyone stopped fucking swearing!" Mum shrieked, then immediately covered her mouth with both hands once she realised what she had said. Despite trying to cover her whole face, I could still see her flush bright red with embarrassment.

"I bet the baby Jesus loved that!" Grandma Flo cackled.

"Oh, shut up, Mother! You're worse than everyone here!" Mum yelled, clearly displeased that things were quickly going off the rails far earlier than usual.

"Don't yell at Grandma!" Craig yelled as he crossed the room to comfort our grandmother, despite the fact she was laughing her arse off at the whole situation.

It was then the whole room erupted into a chaotic squabble as every member of the family voiced their opinion at once. Arguing over who was the most offensive; who needed to stop yelling at who; on whether we should play Trivial Pursuit, or select something a little less... um... volatile. Although, in my mind, I couldn't imagine what game wouldn't be volatile in the hands of these utter whack jobs.

Liam gently grabbed my arm and carefully pulled me away from the ensuing melee, smiling like the insanity unfolding around us was all perfectly reasonable. I suppose compared to his own family, mine was positively healthy and functional. Maybe Uncle Jack wasn't the only one who should be in therapy.

"Merry Christmas, my love," Liam said as he brought me in for a gentle kiss. And in that moment, all the lunacy around me melted away as I focused on my husband. I still loved the sound of that. Husband.

"I guess that's everything wrapped up neatly. A typical Nolan Family Christmas, with bonus wedding and abstract craziness." I said, looking into Liam's eyes.

"There's just one thing I still want to know." Liam said carefully, "What exactly were you caught doing in the shed when you were fifteen?"

Bugger I thought he'd forgotten about that. This called for a distraction. I smiled at him enigmatically.

"You know what, Mum?" I called out, without looking away from Liam, "On second thoughts, Trivial Pursuit sounds like a great idea. Liam said he wants to go first!"

Liam's eyes went wide and he gulped as I grinned evilly at him. Mum dashed off to grab the board game as the rest of the room groaned, knowing exactly what was about to unfold.

"Damn, whatever it was you did must have been really bad. Especially if you're willing to throw your own husband under the bus just to avoid spilling the beans." Liam said breathlessly, sounding almost impressed at my staggering monstrousness.

I picked up the dice from the coffee table where Mum was setting up the game board. I handed them to Liam and carefully pushed him toward his ultimate fate.

"I love you," I whispered in his ear, as he gulped again.

I resolved to tell him everything later. But first, I wanted to watch him squirm and suffer.

After all, it was Christmas.

THE END

Follow Alex Leslie on Social Media

X (formally Twitter): http://www.x.com/alexleslie

Threads: @alexleslieauthor@threads.net

Facebook: http://www.facebook.com/alexleslieauthor

Instagram: http://www/instagram.com/alexleslieauthor

Website: http://www.alexleslieauthor.com

Other Books by Alex Leslie

- MEN OF MELBOURNE -
Chasing The Cupcake Boy
Christmas With The Cupcake Boy
Hearts Unfrozen
- THE NOLAN FAMILY -
My Big Gay Family Christmas Fiasco
My Big Gay Family Christmas Wedding Disaster
- STAND ALONE TITLES -
Following His Bliss

Don't miss out!

Visit the website below and you can sign up to receive emails whenever Alex Leslie publishes a new book. There's no charge and no obligation.

https://books2read.com/r/B-A-CCJI-VTDAF

BOOKS 2 READ

Connecting independent readers to independent writers.

Also by Alex Leslie

MEN OF MELBOURNE
Chasing The Cupcake Boy
Christmas With The Cupcake Boy
Hearts Unfrozen

The Nolan Family
My Big Gay Family Christmas Fiasco
My Big Gay Family Christmas Wedding Disaster

Standalone
Following His Bliss

Watch for more at www.alexleslieauthor.com.

About the Author

Alex Leslie is an Australian-born author of Gay M/M romance works including *Chasing The Cupcake Boy*, *Hearts Unfrozen*, *Following His Bliss* and *My Big Gay Family Christmas Fiasco*.

Alex lives with his partner, two troublesome cats (who love sleeping on his laptop!) and is currently dealing with an ongoing addiction to iced coffee drinks.

Read more at www.alexleslieauthor.com.